COOPER'S FOLLY

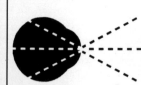

COOPER'S FOLLY

MARY STRAND

THORNDIKE PRESS
A part of Gale, Cengage Learning

GALE
CENGAGE Learning·

Farmington Hills, Mich • San Francisco • New York • Waterville, Maine
Meriden, Conn • Mason, Ohio • Chicago

GALE
CENGAGE Learning

LIBRARY OF CONGRESS CATALOGING-IN-PUBLICATION DATA

Strand, Mary.
  Cooper's Folly / by Mary Strand.
    pages cm. — (Thorndike Press Large Print Clean Reads)
    ISBN-13: 978-1-4104-7187-1 (hardcover)
    ISBN-10: 1-4104-7187-X (hardcover)
    1. Nannies—Fiction. 2. Love stories. 3. Large type books. I. Title.
  PS3619.T738C66 2014
  813'.6—dc23   2014018446

Published in 2014 by arrangement with BelleBooks, Inc.

Printed in Mexico
1 2 3 4 5 6 7 18 17 16 15 14

For Tom, who bought me DramaticaPro
and told me to go for it, and the kidlets,
who smile indulgently every time I do.

CHAPTER ONE

Minneapolis lawyer goes berserk, yells "handle your own freaking cases" at senior partners, grabs fishing pole, and runs into the seventy-five-degree sunshine known as a Minnesota summer. Last seen with a keg of beer and a pickup truck with bumper sticker, I QUIT.

Fantasies. Cooper Meredith had them.

Three o'clock. No, to be precise, it was 3:06. Another endless Friday afternoon.

Cooper leaned back in his burgundy leather chair and scowled at the antique gold clock on his desk. Seeking a second opinion, he turned to his Rolex, then to the grandfather clock in the far corner of his office. No luck. Exactly two and nine-tenths billable hours until he had a hope of slipping away without raising the eyebrows of senior partners. And then only two more working days until Monday — which was more a reality than a joke at the one-hundred-and-eighty-lawyer firm of Pemberton, Smith and Garrison.

Note to the file: Destroy all clocks.

Idly, Cooper imagined his mother's white-gloved, horrified expression at the vision of her precious Bulova smashed beyond recognition at the hands of a crazed, hammer-wielding junior partner. *Sources at the firm said Meredith took off a black wingtip and bashed a Bulova clock on his desk while shouting, "I never wanted to be a lawyer, Mom. I wanted to run a waterski shop on Lake Minnetonka!"* Wincing, he admitted certain defeat once again at the hands of Mom's elegant ambitions for him. Back to the drawing board.

A trial lawyer at Pemberton, Cooper had already argued several cases before the Supreme Court at the ripe old age of thirty-four. That level of success had come at a steep price. His personal life, this thing called a "life" in general, no longer existed, but he still remembered his old life. Leaning back, arms behind his head, legs strewn across the one bare patch of wood on his desk, Cooper drifted back to long-ago summers when the piles were of dirt, when intense negotiations meant convincing Mom that he *needed* a new bike, when the hardest task he faced every day was skimming barefoot behind a speedboat on Lake Minnetonka without crashing.

"Coop!"

Flinching at the interruption, he looked up to see his best friend, Jake Weaver, slouched in the doorway. Even after all these years, Jake still claimed he could satisfy endless legal issues, women, and other pursuits with time to spare — and he somehow did. But how? By not making partner, for one thing. By settling for just good enough.

"Let's cut out early and grab a beer at the Blue Saloon."

"Sorry. I have to put the finishing touches on the brief for the Hadley case. One stray comma, and Garrison goes berserk. You know how he is. My weekend is toast."

"You already made partner, Coop, and the Hadley case will still be here a year from now. Who cares? Live a little. I hear Betsy's been asking about you. Not many guys would pass up that opportunity."

"Tell you what. Do us both a favor and seize that opportunity for yourself." Cooper could picture the reaction of Betsy Vickerman — a stunning brunette lawyer in a competing firm whose curves, brains, and ego were off the charts — if she heard him offer her up to Jake.

When reached for comment at Meredith's

9

*Lake Minnetonka summer house, fellow law-
yer and brunette stunner Betsy "The Bomb"
Vickerman could only fan herself and stagger
outside long enough to say, "Coop was worth
the wait."*

Shaking his head to clear that thought, Coop caught Jake's bemused gaze and wished he hadn't.

"Coop, you're killing yourself. Life isn't about Garrison or clients or, for Pete's sake, the latest Supreme Court opinion. Since when did an 'all-nighter' mean staring at a computer screen, and not having a sweet pair of legs wrapped around you until sunrise? You've left the old Coop behind somewhere — knowing you, probably waiting to be filed alphabetically."

Cooper stood, turning his back on his friend as he stared out at the Minneapolis skyline from the forty-seventh floor of the Healey Building, one of the best views in downtown Minneapolis. What was wrong with him? Work. Seven days a week, twelve to twenty hours a day, killing himself over pointless cases for ungrateful clients. "I just can't stop the flow of work. Garrison keeps dumping it on me while he runs out and plays golf. I'm so pissed off, I could wrap a golf club around his —"

As if on cue, Thomas Garrison appeared

in Cooper's doorway. Silver haired and silver tongued, his skills as a rainmaker kept the Pemberton firm rolling in clients and Cooper buried in lawsuits. Without fail, a visit from Garrison meant more unwanted work, half of it something a kid in the mail room could do. Stiffening, Cooper mourned the lack of a trapdoor underneath his desk.

Too late to run. Too late to hide.

"Good work on that petition yesterday, Meredith. Impressive. With your attention to detail, I've decided to let you take my place in the trial lawyers' writing forum. As secretary, you'll gather and edit every lawyer's bio, but we're only talking a couple hundred lawyers. I've, er, let that task slide for a year or so, and it's due Monday, but I'm sure you'll have no trouble fitting it in with your caseload."

Unbelievable. Cooper glanced at Jake, who rolled his eyes.

"I appreciate the honor, Tom, but I don't have the time —"

"Excellent. Glad to hear it, Meredith." Without waiting to hear more, Tom Garrison ambled down the hall, another load off his desk and on someone else's.

Cooper threw his stapler at the wall, nailing his framed law-school diploma. The glass shattered and landed all over the floor.

It pretty much summed up his attitude.

Jake snorted. "The old guy hasn't lost his touch. Speaking of which, if we can get you out in the boat next weekend, I'll bet you haven't lost your touch with lunker bass. You need a break, Coop. Come on."

"You heard Garrison. I'm in a hole so deep, I won't be able to dig myself out until next year."

His gut clenching, Cooper stared without blinking down at his black wingtips, then at the patterns in the parquet floor. He wished a hole would appear and swallow him. Not that there was much of him left to swallow. "The senior partners here think they own me. Do this. Do that. Get my lunch. Tie my shoes. No mistakes, but if I do something great it just means more work. When I divide my salary by the hours I'm putting in, I might as well be making minimum wage."

Not waiting for Jake's certain comeback, Cooper kept going, raising his hands in surrender. "And why bother? Is there some real person we help? It's always a big corporation that doesn't know I exist, not the poor unfortunates we talked about in law school." He felt like he'd been doing this forty years, not nine. "It's not fun anymore."

"When was it ever fun? The problem is

12

you always saw practicing law as part of you. It's just a job. Maybe it pays better than some other careers, but my life doesn't depend on this place. Yours shouldn't, either."

Glancing at the *Star Tribune* tossed on his desk, Cooper's eyes burned with an intensity he hadn't allowed even Jake to glimpse in a while. He felt his spine stiffen, something it hadn't done — at least around Tom Garrison — in way too long. "Jake, you're absolutely right. I'm tired of being Garrison's whipping boy, tired of doing this, tired of everything. You can have the money. I'm getting out."

Jake sputtered, spilling the cup of coffee in his hand. "Wh-what are you talking about? I didn't tell you to quit, just to find some balance. Take a vacation. Ask for a few weeks' or a couple months' sabbatical. Say you're taking care of family issues. Health issues. Whatever. All you need is a hobby, or a new woman, or —"

Cooper, squaring his shoulders, glowered at Jake. "I've been unhappy here since . . . well, forever. I worked like a dog all those years to get into a top firm and make partner, and for what? More work? No, this is the best idea I've had in way too long."

Jake's eyes grew wide. "Coop, you —"

Cooper slashed a hand through the air to cut off Jake's argument. "The classifieds are filled with jobs. I've got money saved, but I don't want to blow through it if I don't have to. I just need enough to get by until I figure out what I'm going to do with my life. I've wasted enough time here."

"What *are* you going to do? What's the rush?"

"It's time. At this point, I'd take pretty much any job that pays okay, sounds easy, and gives me some semblance of a life. Maybe just for the summer. With all those degrees I have, it should be a snap."

Leaning over his desk, Cooper opened the newspaper to the classifieds, perusing column after column. Teaching. Insurance. Marketing. Telemarketing. Sales. Domestic work. Outdoor work. Health care. Childcare. The list was endless.

Jabbing his finger at the ads, Cooper looked up at Jake. "Whatever my finger hit just now, I'm doing it. I'm going back out there and doing something that makes me happy. A job is just a job."

"You can't be serious." Jake slammed the door to Coop's office before striding over to him and grabbing him by the shoulders. "Talk to me, Coop. This is a joke, right?"

Cooper shook him off. "Whatever job my

finger is on, that's what I'm going for."

He grinned. This was the first impulsive thing he'd done since fifth grade, when he'd eaten a spider and promptly threw up all over Mrs. Josifek, who took a leave of absence for a month.

Ignoring Jake and the look he knew was plastered all over his friend's face, Coop glanced down at his finger — at the words printed beneath his finger — and tried not to think about whether he was making the mistake of a lifetime. He'd know soon enough.

Practically since birth, Cooper's mom had drilled into him that the "right" life was stuffy, conservative, and focused on law and financial success. Everything else was "folly." Until the word "folly" made him want to cover his ears and scream. Until, finally, "folly" became the exact opposite of him.

He couldn't wait to tell Mom what he was about to do.

Not.

The law firm of Pemberton, Smith and Garrison confirms that junior partner Cooper Meredith has left the firm following recent erratic behavior including assaulting a clock, telling senior partners to perform certain physically impossible acts on themselves, and

*leaving for Lake Minnetonka with what Mere-
dith referred to as beer, gear, and Betsy "The
Bomb" Vickerman.*

*In related news, Meredith is currently re-
ported to be seeking work as a nanny.*

CHAPTER TWO

Molly Perrell paused, frowning, as she hung up the phone. That was odd. Something . . . unusual . . . about this nanny, but she couldn't put her finger on it. *Sheesh. You're analyzing everything to death. Forget about it.*

Her Manolos tapping out a staccato beat on the tiled kitchen floor, Molly continued to ponder, unable to stop her mental gyrations. She had received an incredible number of applicants in response to her ad. Which was good. There were a lot of crazies, incompetents, and just plain losers out there in the world, many of whom seemed to be applying for the job as her nanny. Which was not so good.

Nannies who couldn't drive. Or couldn't speak English, let alone read even the simplest books to Alec and Emma. Or didn't like children. Or were still children themselves. Or seemed to have problems with lying, stealing, and things she didn't want to think about, much less read about in their criminal records. Or had the sort of tattoos and piercings they could've only acquired in prison or on a drunken binge. After three weeks of this, Molly had a great deal more respect for the people in her personnel office, who put up with job applicants like these on a daily basis.

She could place another ad. Same results, probably. Try that agency again? They struck out the last time, but maybe she'd just had bad luck. A lot of her friends had sung their praises. With the fee they charged, they *ought* to be good. The fee didn't matter so much — she'd gladly pay it for the right nanny — but the agency was always swamped with households needing a nanny, especially in the summer. It took at least a month to get a decent one. Maybe longer.

Running her hands through her hair for what seemed like the hundredth time that day, Molly stopped her pacing and sank into the nearest chair. She had hoped to have a nanny a week ago. What on earth was she going to do?

The one time she asked a big favor of her ex, he'd actually promised to take the kids during her New York trip this week. She was such a fool to believe him. To trust him. Drew had broken yet another promise. This time, he'd done it too late to allow her time to find an alternative.

After firing her last nanny, an ex-military woman who'd been so charming in her interview but less charming after she showed the kids how to waterboard their "enemies," Molly had struggled to cobble together a patchwork quilt of childcare for the twins. Her luck had ended yesterday with Drew's call.

This latest candidate sounded so good on paper. Almost too good. Shuffling through the pile of applications that arrived yesterday, Molly lingered on the neatly typed letter on crisp, ivory stationery. *Meredith Cooper.*

Everything about this woman seemed exceptional. Education, references, employment. Molly hadn't heard of Pemberton — although the name sounded familiar — but it appeared to be a day-care facility. This nanny candidate, Meredith, had worked there for nine years and spoke glowingly about the experience she'd gained. It sounded like she worked more with babies, but she also mentioned mediating a number of disputes. Among children? Meredith was looking for shorter hours in her next experience, but that didn't sound like a problem based on the horrendous hours she said she'd been putting in.

It was a little odd, though, that Meredith didn't sign the application letter but had just typed her name. And so formally. *Cooper, Meredith.* She also described her experience in such a careful, almost legalistic manner. Molly more often saw language like that from the "suits" three floors up at the office, who scouted out and bought new locations for Harrowby's, the large department store chain for which Molly worked as the senior buyer.

Molly had dealt with far stranger applications than this one in the last three weeks — by a long shot — and she couldn't afford to be picky. Especially today.

Another odd thing, though. When Molly called Meredith just now, a distinctly male voice spoke on her answering machine. But who knows? If it didn't affect job performance, Meredith's sleeping arrangements didn't matter. And it might be perfectly explainable. Maybe Meredith had a guy friend record her answering machine message for safety reasons. Some of Molly's other single friends did that.

Molly leaned back in the chair, crossing and uncrossing her legs distractedly as she replayed in her mind the answering machine message. "Hi. You've reached me. Leave a message. I'll call." There was something elemental about that man. Strong, sure of himself, to the point. Yet, at the same time, warm, even teasing. Suggestive. *Virile,* as Brooke, her next-door neighbor, was forever saying about some man or another.

Molly rolled her eyes at the thought of Brooke, who had too much time on her hands these days. *Get a grip, Molly.* Since when did she start losing it over a few words on an answering machine?

In any case, she didn't have the time or energy to think about a man right now. Her flight left at nine-thirty tomorrow morning, and Molly desperately needed a nanny. Today.

Crossing her fingers for luck, she hoped Meredith was the miracle she'd been praying for.

Three o'clock. Cooper checked the time, the address, then his reflection in the rearview mirror. Somehow, he had to shake that deer-in-the-headlights look, or he would never pull this off. *Suck it up, Coop.*

What the heck. He wouldn't be going back to Pemberton.

After yanking up the parking brake, Cooper opened the door of his torch-red Corvette convertible and unfolded himself from the car. He sure wouldn't be able to buy this car on a nanny's salary. But he'd already paid for it and, for that matter, every other toy he could ever need or want. How happy did any of that make him?

Okay, the convertible made him happy, especially on a gorgeous, sunny, blue-sky day like today. But the nanny job didn't need to pay well enough to buy him this little beauty. He already owned it.

He reminded himself, again, that this whole nanny gig was a joke. A lark. Something he'd bragged to Jake he could do. He *wouldn't* go back to Pemberton, but after treating himself to one carefree summer, he'd be ready for something serious again.

Serious but less soul-sucking.

Cooper shook his head, stretched, and cast a cursory glance over the neighborhood. The Morningside neighborhood of Edina, just past the western edge of Minneapolis, definitely had a suburban feel, but it wasn't so far from the urban hub of Minneapolis that he felt like he'd completely left civilization for the boonies. Morningside was a quick fifteen-minute drive — at least, when Cooper was driving — from his high-rise condo in Loring Park on the fringes of downtown Minneapolis. For all the differences, though, it might as well be two hours.

Cooper loved his condo and his neighborhood. Downtown, hip, cosmopolitan — part of the young, money-to-burn, urban professional world, surrounded by more theaters, restaurants, bars, and stores than anyone could ever find time for. Lately, though, thoughts of green grass, trees, lakes, and wide-open spaces had flitted through his brain.

Morningside's lush trees graced almost-too-manicured lawns that smelled of lilacs, roses, and freshly mowed grass. Wide, clean streets filled with kids laughing, playing ball, pausing only for the passing of an occasional minivan or sport utility vehicle or, in Cooper's case, sports car. The five- and six-bedroom, ivy-draped Colonials everywhere he looked, with three-car garages and more than a few swimming pools, looked more like mansions than houses.

To Cooper, it also looked like what he'd known growing up. If his next job took him here, he could get used to it.

He glanced up sharply at the sound of birds chirping in the trees and sky above him. They weren't chirping "folly, folly," were they?

No. Of course not. Shaking his head, he stepped across the boulevard and strolled up the front sidewalk to the massive front entrance of the Perrell home. He commanded his stomach to stop jumping as he glimpsed the backyard swimming pool and state-of-the-art tree house beyond an open gate, scanned the endless toys and balls scattered throughout the yard, and observed a high-pitched screech coming from the general direction of the tree house.

Wait . . . screech? No, the ad clearly said this woman had two happy kids, which left out screeching ones, so some neighbor kid must be using the tree house. Cooper didn't mind signing on for a couple of easy, happy kids, so with any luck he wouldn't have to spend much time watching the bratty neighbor kids who liked hanging out in this tree house. He would have to be clear about that with Ms. Perrell. After she gave him the job.

Willing but unable to postpone the moment of truth, Cooper took an extra second to brush back a perpetually stubborn blond lock from his forehead, then rang the doorbell. The chime echoed throughout the house. Before the echo faded — before he had time to come to his senses and run, not walk, back to his car — the *rat-a-tat-tat* of either a machine gun or an impatient woman's heels exploded down the entry hall.

Preparing to do battle with either, Cooper

plastered his best aw-shucks, you-can-trust-me smile on his face. For once in his life, he wished he'd taken more time to observe the ultra-smooth Jake Weaver in action with women. Cooper had never lacked for skills in the courtroom, but he had a feeling he was in over his head in this situation.

The machine-gun heels came to an abrupt halt, giving way to the screen door wildly swinging open and prompting Cooper to take a nimble step back from the fast-approaching doorknob. Mesmerized by the bright red pumps that almost caused him to jump out of his own shoes, Cooper recollected his purpose for being there and brought his gaze north of her shoes. Slowly.

Long, willowy legs that could stop traffic — at least, if he were driving. Short, but not short enough, sundress with a wide red belt accentuating a surprisingly thin waist. Farther north, thin shoulder straps performing a small feat in holding up the dress and its contents. A neck that seemed to reach for the stars, although it ended abruptly at the base of the most stunning face Cooper had ever seen. Red lips, aristocratic nose, and wide-set, flashing eyes in the deepest shade of emerald. The vision was completed by frothy, pale blond hair he usually saw only on a kid, cut in one of those short, professional styles that, on this woman, somehow triggered a completely *un*professional reaction in him.

Cooper blinked, clearing his head. He'd maybe been expecting a comfortably attractive, friendly-looking mom with dirty handprints on her jeans and messed-up hair, a woman distracted and disheveled by rambunctious, out-of-control kids. This mom looked like she could've just stepped off the pages of one of Cooper's own mom's fashion magazines. She had five-foot-long legs that cried out an invitation and flashing eyes that —

Were flashing, impatiently, at Cooper.

"I'm so sorry, really, but I don't have the time for whatever you're selling. I have a busy schedule. Thanks. Have a good day." The woman didn't look the least bit sorry as she tried without success to shut the door. She looked at the end of her rope.

Cooper's left knee — yeah, the one he'd impulsively stuck in the door when it started to swing shut — throbbed. He weighed the pros and cons of extricating his leg, debating whether any job, let alone this one, was worth the amputation of a limb, not to mention the embarrassment of having his pals know the size of the foe who'd done the

26

damage.

Reaching any decision was difficult, of course, when the woman on the other side of the screen door left him feeling a little bit stupid. And, oddly, quite a bit outmatched.

Finally recollecting that his opponents in court admired his gift for out-talking anyone, anywhere, Cooper pulled himself together. Sort of. Certainly, this couldn't be PS and G's finest trying to string together a simple noun and verb? After all, until this agonizing moment, he'd had full command of the entire English language and a healthy chunk of Latin, too.

A sudden stabbing pain behind his right knee saved Cooper from further meandering through the wasteland that, in the last couple minutes, his mind had become.

Just as he acknowledged that he would never walk — or talk — again, the screen door flew open and hit his leg as well. Cooper staggered backward from the sudden and unexpected return of his left leg, tripped, and sprawled against a porch rail. Two wild monkeys leaped on top of him. One playfully threw her arms around his right pants leg, threatening to hug it to death, while the other climbed up his left thigh and began bouncing tennis balls off Cooper's stomach while he kept asking if

Coop knew how to play catch. When the woman pried them off, Cooper regained his feet. Regaining his dignity? Not so fast.

"Mom-meeee!" The female urchin began to shriek and clung, trembling, to the woman, who had long since abandoned the protection of the screen door. "Is this man trying to hurt you?"

"No, sweetie, of course not. But thanks for protecting me so well." The woman — Ms. Perrell? — softened her voice as she spoke to the little girl. The soothing tone sure wasn't the same as the one with which she'd greeted Cooper.

The little girl beamed at her mom's praise. The clinging and trembling slowed but didn't stop completely.

The little boy, meanwhile, squeezed the tennis ball in his chubby little fist and declared that Cooper must not know how to play baseball. Amused, Cooper reflected that a few of his opponents in court would've liked to taunt him like that without fear of reprisal.

His miniature opponent appeared quite thoughtful about Cooper, sizing him up as if for battle, despite assurances from Ms. Perrell that he wasn't a "bad man." *Hell, how does she know?* Did he look like a wimp, totally incapable of inflicting harm?

Well, yeah, maybe, if these two squirts were able to handle him so easily.

Busy grinning at the two little kids, Cooper didn't hear the woman's question until she repeated it a second time. Or maybe a third.

"What is it that you want? I have an appointment, and I just don't have the time to deal with anything else today. Is it something that could wait until another day, Mr. . . . ?"

Now or never. "Meredith. Cooper Meredith. But I believe your appointment is with me, so hopefully it won't have to wait until another day." Cooper beamed his most affable smile her way, to counteract his otherwise pathetic opening. He suspected, though, that the look of stark disbelief plastered on Ms. Perrell's face was mirrored on his own. By some miracle, his legs remained standing, and both kids were awestruck in blissful silence.

It didn't occur to Cooper until moments later that the kids' awe wasn't focused on him, as he had first assumed, but on the sight of someone successfully baffling their mother. At about the same time, he realized that these pint-sized, hyper, semiprofessional wrestlers were the four-year-old twins this delusional woman referred to in her ad as "practically perfect."

Cute and protective of their mom and probably in need of some serious sugar detox, yes. Practically perfect, no.

Was it too late to retract his resignation? What had he done? Why had he ignored Jake's irritatingly sage advice? And how quickly could he find the nearest escape route?

Out of the corner of his eye, Cooper noticed the boy nudge the girl, as the girl giggled in a high-pitched little titter. The boy's eyes roamed over Cooper now, pretending an impassive, even blasé, gaze that was undone now by almost frenzied nudging. The girl stared in fascination. Cooper fought the urge to look down at his shirt to see if part of his lunch had managed to land there. He didn't need to wonder long.

"Mommy, he's cute, and you said he's not a bad man. Do you like him? Can he come play with us? Does he like hot dogs? Can he stay? Does Uncle Steve like him, too?"

The woman, roused to her senses by the incessant stream of questions voiced by the little girl, finally interrupted the interrogation. "Emma. Alec. Go inside, please. I need to speak to this man, and then he'll be leaving. You can play in the tree house again later."

No movement from the troops, who continued to stare at Cooper, spellbound. At least the questions stopped. Something to be grateful for, he supposed. So far, that appeared to be a rarity around here. Meanwhile, the queasy feeling in the pit of Cooper's stomach grew, with three pairs of emerald eyes now trained on him.

He winced as a slight groan escaped, killing all hopes of faking the confidence it took to bluff his way into this job. His only remaining hope was to leave with what remained of his dignity — if not his knees — intact.

Ms. Perrell's look hadn't changed, unless it was growing even more irritated than it had started out. "You heard me, Emma and Alec. Inside. Now. No more stalling."

She had more control over them than Cooper had suspected. With one last peek at him, they headed inside. And stood, still peering at him, on the other side of the screen door, threatening to push their noses or their chubby little hands right through it if they pressed any harder. Ms. Perrell sent them into the living room and shut the inside door. From the look on her face, it wasn't so she could have a chance to get to know him better.

"Listen, I'm sorry about the kids. They, um, like to play. But I was expecting Meredith Cooper at three o'clock. You show up and tell me you're Cooper Meredith. I'm looking for a nanny, not . . ." Her eyes perused him from head to toe, and he could've sworn she sighed. As in, she didn't mind looking — and, yeah, the feeling was mutual — but maybe not on a Sunday afternoon when she obviously needed a nanny. She ran a hand through her hair, staring past him now. "I don't know what to say. Is this a joke? A prank someone's playing? I have to travel out of town tomorrow for work. I can't cancel my trip."

"I'm not —"

She held up a hand. "I'm just trying to be honest. It's been a tough day, and I wasn't expecting this." Her gaze caught his and lingered on his eyes and mouth a moment too long before darting away again. "I'm sorry. Really. I wasn't expecting *you.*"

"Look, Ms. Perrell. You're jumping to a lot of conclusions. Let me explain." Beads of sweat trickled down Cooper's forehead, removing all hope of passing himself off as the confident man he once was. A lifetime ago. Maybe this morning.

"I'll give you five minutes, Mr. Meredith." This time she definitely sighed. "Go for it."

Molly had no idea what this man could possibly want. He seemed respectable and even harmless — although you never could tell these days — but he must have an ulterior motive, right? Was Drew playing a joke on her? No, that didn't make sense, especially after he'd dumped on her like this at the last minute.

Drew hadn't cared enough about her or the kids when they were still married to bother with a practical joke. He didn't even exert himself enough to claim his weekend visitation rights with the kids, since it might interfere with his flavor-of-the-week girlfriend. No. This whole thing didn't make sense.

Her eyes took another quick sweep of him. Gorgeous. She'd always been a sucker for those tall surfer-blonds with the big, sky-blue eyes, and one was standing right in front of her. On the slim side, with broad shoulders that seemed frozen into a careless shrug. She knew the type. The guy exuded confidence. So like Drew, and yet . . . not at all.

Well, no time for this now, unfortunately, even if a guy who looked like he did would ever take a second glance at her. Anyway, she needed a nanny, not a stud, and she needed one today.

Those amazing blue eyes looked sincere.

Hard to believe. "I'm sorry you're upset. All I'm here for is a job interview." As he paused, he wiped his hands on his slacks. "I'd hoped if you met me, you'd give me a shot."

"Wait a minute. This isn't a joke? You're serious about this job?" Reeling from the new twist in what she had assumed was someone's idea of a practical joke, Molly's brain finally registered, almost as an after-thought, the rest of his words. He wanted a shot. Almost as if he were desperate for work, despite what the labels on his clothes and the car parked in front of Molly's house told her. "What, or who, are you?"

He thrust out the palms of both hands, as if to halt her.

"Hey, if I'm stuck having to make my case in five minutes, you've got to stop the cross-exam."

His impulsive response amused her, and she spared him a grin. "Fair point, counselor. You get two more minutes."

His self-assured demeanor slipped a bit as he reflexively straightened his nonexistent tie. Pretty funny, actually, since he wore a casual polo shirt. "How'd you know I'm a lawyer?"

Her grin became a grimace as shock dawned into comprehension. Oh, God. This

34

was worse than she'd thought. Had Drew sent a lawyer to check up on her?

No. Impossible.

Drew wasn't a cheapskate and never had complained for a moment about the financial burdens of supporting his kids. So much for her first theory. Well, it had to be something. It always did. But why did it have to happen to her, and when there was no time to deal with it?

As Molly pondered the situation, the fates, and why they seemed to have it out for her, Cooper Meredith's voice interrupted her thoughts.

"Anyway, yeah, I'm a lawyer. Or used to be."

Still lost in thought, Molly only faintly registered his words.

When she didn't say anything, he continued. "I practiced at the Pemberton law firm downtown for the last nine years. Although I did pretty well there, I realized it didn't give me what I want out of life. I saw your ad and thought it sounded like a perfect opportunity for a guy who loves kids and would relish the chance to have a hand, as a caregiver and maybe even a role model, in the lives of a couple of 'bright, happy' children."

The "bright, happy" words from the ad

she'd placed weren't lost on her. If the guy wanted a job, he sure didn't show it. But Molly's dilemma was acute. She couldn't imagine anyone leaving a high-powered law firm to babysit her kids. There was obviously a story there. On the other hand, her gut told her that he was an okay guy. No experience with kids, she'd bet, but not someone who would harm them or burn down the house. And she still had time today to check his references and make sure he was on the level.

More pressing, at least right this moment, Molly had no other prospects whatsoever for a nanny, and she was booked on the nine-thirty flight to LaGuardia in the morning. If she had to cancel that trip, she'd be in deep trouble with her boss at Harrowby's. She hoped she wouldn't regret this.

"Do you have any experience with children? Do you have any idea what you're in for?" If the guy wasn't at least honest, Molly would have to let go of her rash idea, no matter how much it wrecked her travel plans or what it cost her at work. But maybe this could be salvageable.

His eyes riveted on hers. Held them. Molly was the first to blink. "Frankly, Ms. Perrell, most of my experience with children came when I was in high school and college. Camp counselor, youth leader at church, sailing and waterski instructor, babysitter to a million cousins. I have references. I also spend some time with my married friends' kids, but the truth is, in the last several years I haven't been able to do much that didn't involve work. Not with kids, not even with adults. I don't want a life like that. That's why I need this change. This is what I want to do."

The truth? Probably. Or close to it. She couldn't dismiss him out of hand, certainly, even if those were just interview lines the guy had picked up in law school. Maybe she ought to throw him out in the street, but she needed him. He probably knew it.

Molly reviewed her options one last time. Unfortunately, she had just one. This man. This — okay — tall, very attractive, very blond, very tempting man. The guy had the most beautiful blue eyes, with flecks of gold, reminding her of the sky on a hazy August day at the lake. Hips slim enough to slide her arms around. The hint of contoured muscles under his shirt that gave him an indefinable sense of power. Of strength. The type of man her next-door neighbor, Brooke, would eat for lunch. And dinner, and most definitely breakfast.

Molly had neither the time nor the tolerance for casual or even not-so-casual flings, but she appreciated a gorgeous man when she saw one. She wasn't dead yet. Cooper Meredith was clearly not dead yet, either. What had Emma said? Oh, yeah — cute. Very cute. More Saturday-night-date material than nanny material, but maybe she could make this work until she got home from New York. With a little help from her sister-in-law and a little luck.

She drew in a long breath and slowly let it out. Paused. Made her decision. "If, and I mean *if,* your references check out in the next few hours, you've gotten yourself a temporary job. I'll just have to pray nothing goes wrong. You start tomorrow morning at seven-thirty sharp. I'm leaving then to catch a flight, and I'll be in New York until Thursday afternoon. We'll revisit the wisdom of this then, when I've had time to think and after you've weathered a few days of 'children's law.' Your hours this week are seven-thirty to six. My sister-in-law, Nancy, will take the kids every night while I'm gone, and she'll call you tomorrow to arrange that. If all of that works for you?"

When he nodded, Molly explained the salary and benefits, which she knew were standard. "One more thing, Mr. Meredith. Despite what my ad said, for you, for obvious reasons, this is a 'live-out' position. I hope you understand?"

He replied with just a slight tilt of his eyebrows. Silence. Molly tried to wait him out but couldn't stand the suspense. She needed him. She steeled herself for the inevitable refusal but asked anyway.

"Well, Mr. Meredith? What's your answer?"

"Ms. Perrell, it's a resounding yes."

Giggling and pushing each other away from the second-floor window where their noses had been plastered since their mother sent them inside, two towheaded children chortled with glee.

"A new one! Yeah! A guy, too. He'll do guy stuff with me, not that sissy stuff you always want to do." Alec pumped his chubby fists at the idea and also didn't mind teasing his twin sister, even though it was tough calling her "sissy" without being punched in the mouth.

"And he's so cute! Maybe Mommy will like him a whole lot, and he can stay with us forever and ever." His sister, just as excited about their new nanny, didn't even hit him. "Maybe he'll know how to braid my hair."

She flipped her hand through her hair,

39

which wasn't much longer than his.

"Oh, Emma, don't be such a dope."

CHAPTER THREE

"No, of course I haven't lost my mind, Nancy. I'm just in a tough spot at work right now, with the fall shows almost upon me and Jed Parker on my back over last month's sales figures."

Gulping her morning coffee, Molly wondered, as she had several times in the last few weeks, why the VP for retail operations would hang her out to dry over sales, when she was the head buyer. It didn't make sense, but it wasn't the first thing they'd failed to mention in her MBA program.

Focusing on her new nanny, Molly continued. "Anyway, it's just until Thursday. The guy's credentials say he could probably design a day care for toddler lawyers-in-training and teach torts to ten-year-olds. He's got some experience with kids, but not as a nanny. Still, he ought to be able to last for a few days, and he'll have your number if he runs into trouble. You don't mind, do you?"

Nancy Perrell was married to Molly's brother, Steve, and had two young kids of her own. Although Nancy ran a small jewelry design business out of her home and didn't have to face the nanny crises that hit Molly from time to time, she understood the demands of the retail world from their early days after business school.

She'd also do just about anything for Molly, who had first introduced her to Steve. To hear Nancy tell it, their honeymoon still wasn't over after six glorious years together. Molly was happy for them, of course, but couldn't take credit for it. When she needed a favor from the grateful Nancy, though, she took it. Like now.

"Not at all, doll. Go have fun in New York, get your nails done, and forget all about us dull people in the hinterlands of Minnesota."

Nancy's words, as always, triggered a reaction in her. "Nancy! Fun? I'll be lucky to have five minutes for meals, the way they'll run us through the paces on this trip. Why —" Finally catching the teasing tone of Nancy's voice, Molly realized her sister-in-law had once again set her up for a good-natured ribbing. She broke off in the middle of her automatic response. "You nailed me again, you goof."

The women shared a laugh. Molly was all too aware that Nancy wanted her to lighten up and not take everything so seriously. Good advice, sure, but hard to follow when she had two kids, a tough job, no husband, and the worst possible luck with nannies.

"We'll have it all under control for you, Moll. So get out of town already. Isn't it about time you left to catch your flight? Is the stud there yet? And, no, don't try to deny that one, girlfriend, since I got the full scoop from Emma when she picked up the phone. 'He's really cute, Aunt Nancy. And he likes Mommy a whole lot.' What's the word? Is he as delectable as he sounds?"

Nancy sounded almost breathless with curiosity. Didn't she understand the guy was just her nanny?

"Cooper Meredith is a well-known, highly-respected lawyer. Steve said so himself. He actually sounds sincere about wanting to take a break from his real life, but he's just my nanny. This week, at least. He's not some . . . some rent-a-stud or something."

It had taken only a couple quick calls to Steve last night to confirm the professional scoop on Cooper Meredith. Steve didn't know the guy personally, but he'd heard of him, had even heard from a friend about his abrupt departure from the Pemberton firm. Steve had handled the reference checks himself, taking one load off Molly's shoulders.

"Yes, I've heard all the dry stuff. College. Law school. Blah, blah, blah. As you know perfectly well, that's not what I'm talking about."

So much for blowing one past Nancy. "Fine. I admit he looks pretty much . . . well, fabulous. But he does *not* like me 'a whole lot.' Not after the way I grilled him yesterday. Frankly, I'm surprised he took the job. I can't imagine why he's doing this. It doesn't make sense."

Molly's bewildered musings of last night, after Alec and Emma had dropped from exhaustion, returned briefly, only to surprise her when replaced by a dreamy vision of Cooper's lips hovering over hers for agonizing moments, approaching but never quite touching. *In your dreams, Molly. He's your nanny, for God's sake. And only because you were desperate.*

"Give it up, Moll. For once in your life, go with the flow. Don't analyze it. I'm sure he has his reasons, and it probably won't be long before you discover what they are. I can't believe they're too sinister, though, with such an upstanding guy, so relax about

44

your New York trip, enjoy your cute new nanny, and chill."

The New York trip. Yes, at least for now, Molly didn't have time for heavy-duty analysis. She had a plane to catch, as soon as Cooper showed up and she barreled through a flurry of last-minute instructions for him. "Whatever you say, Nancy. Hey, thanks for doing this. I owe you. See you Thursday, and give that ugly brother of mine a hug."

Hanging up, Molly's mind raced over what she still had to do before leaving. With all the "help" provided by Emma and Alec, who'd both been underfoot since she opened her eyes this morning, she should have no trouble getting away by . . . noon. Smiling, Molly sent the twins back to the kitchen to finish their breakfast for the tenth time in the last half hour.

Not for the first time that morning, Cooper asked himself if he'd lost his mind for bragging to Jake that he could do any job he set his mind to. His elation over getting through the job interview had dulled, leaving him with a vague, unsettled feeling. What had come over him to do something this crazy?

True to form, his mom had already called it folly. At least ten times so far, and he had a feeling she was just warming up.

Jake's fishing trip sounded pretty good right now. Tom Garrison and a long line of demanding, thankless, irritating clients didn't look quite so bad, either. Digging drainage ditches at a leper colony? Not out of the question.

Trouble was, he might have left the practice of law — "for now," all his friends and partners said with those patronizing smirks — but he couldn't for the life of him breach his contract with Ms. Perrell. No matter what, he was still Cooper.

He shrugged into a polo shirt, fastened his belt, and slipped on his loafers. No suit or tie for this job, at least. With a last glance around his condo, he walked out, hurried to his Corvette in the underground ramp, and raced out into the brilliant sunshine of another gorgeous summer day. Top down, wind streaking through his hair, Cooper settled in for an all-too-quick zip around Lake of the Isles before heading west on Excelsior. Gazing up at the cloudless, dazzling sky, he decided it might not be such a bad day after all.

The doorbell chimed a warning at his new employer, who let him cool his heels for a minute on the front porch. He cursed the telltale perspiration already making an appearance on his shirt. Hearing clattering feet, he stood straighter. Showtime.

Peering in through the screen door, his misgivings dissolved as he watched the twins trip over each other in their race to the door. Two pairs of stubby little legs churned in unison, blocking his view of Molly Perrell as she walked toward him. They acted for all the world as if the circus had come to town.

Halted by a shout from their mother, the twins stopped. Once again, the door crashed open, but Cooper was an old pro at this by now and stepped back in time. At the sight of her, he nearly stepped backward again, which would have landed him in the roses that lined the front steps. *Wow.* Cooper had worked with a number of well-dressed female professionals, but Ms. Perrell made them all look like amateurs. Which they were, he figured, if they went head-to-head against the senior buyer at Harrowby's.

He'd spent the evening on the phone with a few friends, hoping to glean whatever info he could about Molly Perrell before walking into her lair. As he had in court, Cooper wanted to know his opponent inside and out before taking her on. He still didn't know much about Ms. Perrell, but she was apparently good at what she did — easy to work with, but tough when she had to be.

Basically, his friends said, she was a lot like him.

She was a showstopper. Interestingly, she didn't look like she was even remotely aware of it. She again wore rat-a-tat-tat heels, this time in a color that matched her eyes. Yesterday's dress was replaced by a sharply cut suit of the same shade of emerald, featuring an almost sinfully short skirt.

Instead of the high-necked blouse Cooper often saw on female colleagues in court, she wore a satiny ivory camisole. Actually, from what he could see of it, it wore *her*. Very well. Based on her clothing, at least, Ms. Perrell was crisp and cool and . . . very hot. A sudden, unquenchable urge to discover whether the interior matched the exterior made Cooper long for a cold shower. Right now.

Trying not to think about her heels or her skirt or her camisole, Coop's gaze shot to her eyes. Stunning, yeah, but tired today. She glanced at her kids with a worried, thoughtful gaze before turning to Cooper.

"Good morning, Mr. Meredith. Thanks for getting here so promptly. I really appreciate it. Now, I have to leave in the next fifteen minutes or so. Why don't I show you around, run through how I do things and the kids' schedules, and give you a few phone numbers in case you have problems." His new boss rattled that off more as a statement than a question, so he figured blind obedience was the desired response. For the moment, he gave it.

She spent the next several minutes doing as promised, reeling through far more instructions than Cooper could possibly need. No problem. He filed it all away in the "for-future-reference" corner of his brain, probably never to be retrieved. If he got really desperate with these two little monkeys, he could always make a phone call to the Minnesota zoo.

Alec, at least, seemed pretty taken with him. He probably didn't see enough men in his life, not if Alec's mom was as cautious with the men she dated as she'd been with Cooper.

Of course, she probably didn't meet a lot of men under quite the same circumstances as she'd met him. Part of him strangely hoped that she didn't meet a lot of men, period. As his nose twitched from the flowery perfume she wore, he figured the odds of that were slim to none.

"Now, I know that's a lot, but it's all written down in the babysitter's book by the kitchen telephone, and you can call Nancy if you have any questions. Make sure you follow the children's meal and nap schedules. I don't want them getting out of their routine. You don't need to worry about bedtime, of course, since Nancy will handle that. Any questions?"

"What —"

"Actually, I have a question." She paused a few long moments as she glanced out the patio doors in the back of the house. At the swimming pool? Up at the sky? "What I still don't understand is why you'd quit one job to take another. I mean, if I had the luxury of quitting . . ." She sighed and turned back to him. "I'd spend a summer next to the pool."

Which might make him her pool boy. There were worse jobs.

He shrugged, still not sure what he wanted to do. "I just knew I needed a change."

Even if it turned out to be temporary.

She nodded, as if she might actually understand — unlike everyone else he knew — and drew a long breath, letting it out slowly. "I've left my number in New York and my cell phone number. Call me if any problems come up that Nancy and you can't handle, but hopefully there won't be any. I'll call the kids every night. They'll be staying at Nancy's and Steve's house, but it's just a few blocks away, and Nancy will have them back here by seven-thirty every morning. Okay?"

This time, she waited for him to nod.

"Thanks again. I've already told the kids goodbye. I have to run, but I'll see you all on Thursday."

With that, the emerald heels and accompanying package disappeared into the garage, and she hopped into her dusky silver BMW sedan, leaving the Mercedes SUV behind for Cooper and the kids. *Cars to go with the clothes,* Cooper thought as he spied her racing down Battery Lane to the stop sign at the corner. But she didn't strike him as vain. She was more —

Practical.

Stressed to the max.

Intriguing.

A wild scream punctured Cooper's brief daydream. From the titter that followed, and the tiny pair of emerald eyes peering up at him through a halo of short blond curls, Cooper deduced that Emma was on the warpath, and he was her primary target. The fact that her chubby but effective little arms had his knees in a death grip was a bonus clue. The reason for her attachment was yet to be discovered.

"Mommy said we could go on a pony ride this morning, Mr. Mertle. Do you have a pony? That's okay, we can go visit the place near my friend Patty. They have lots and lots of ponies. Some of them are even bigger than you. Do you like ponies, Mr. Merfish? My mommy likes them a lot, and she'd really like us to go ride them."

The skill of one so little in batting her eyelashes amazed him, while he highly doubted the pony bit.

"Let's call up your mom and ask her if it's okay." Cooper figured that would stop the little rogue dead in her tracks. He wasn't prepared for a four-year-old's cunning.

"Mommy will be really, really mad at you if you bother her at work, Mr. Mertis. She might yell and come home and spank you. She never spanks me. That's 'cause I'm a good girl, and I never call her at work. She likes ponies. She said so when she 'splained everything to you, but you weren't listening good. Were you looking at her? She's pretty. Do you like Mommy? Could we go now? I don't want the ponies all gone. Then Mommy will be sad, 'cause I'll be sad, and she'll be really mad."

Not even eight on my first morning, and we're talking pony rides. At this rate, he'd be launching the kids in a rocket to the moon by Wednesday. Hmmm. Not such a bad idea. Cooper had thirty years on this pint-sized negotiator. She was good, but she hadn't seen one of the top litigators from PS and G in action. "Okay, Emma. We'll go for a pony ride after I call your aunt Nancy and tell her about it. It sounds so fun, I bet she'll want to go too, don't you think?"

Emma didn't easily concede defeat. "Aunt Nancy is gone right now. She told me so this morning. She'll be gone for a real long time, maybe an hour. I don't think you can find her anywhere, and her phone sometimes doesn't answer when I call it. I like to call her, but baby Charlie sleeps a lot, and Mommy says the phone wakes him up. Charlie isn't a big kid like me, so he takes lots of naps. I never take naps. But I like donuts. Do you like donuts, Mr. Merdish? Aunt Nancy does. But don't worry — I'll tell her about the ponies later. She's really, really busy now. I'm ready to go."

During her spellbinding oration, Cooper stood, mesmerized, clearly outdone. Meanwhile, Emma dragged out her shoes as she spoke, calmly putting them on and fastening the Velcro straps before marching to the door leading into the garage, car keys in hand. She had no doubt of her audience, or of the verdict.

Cooper sighed. It was going to be a long week, but it looked to be interesting. There would be more battles ahead with Emma. With practice, he might even win one. Of course, while he was preoccupied with her, he hadn't seen what Alec could do to him. Yet.

Another thing was clear. "Mr. Meredith" was too big a mouthful for four-year-olds. "You win, Emma. We'll go ride ponies. But, kid, call me 'Cooper,' okay?"

Emma answered with a gleeful squeal as she sashayed out the door. Cooper rounded up Alec and, moments later, followed.

Pony rides weren't on the list of instructions Molly had given Cooper, as he well knew. Swimming at Lake Harriet, flying newly bought kites in the park, gobbling ice-cream cones, and shrieking through every ride at Nickelodeon Universe in the Mall of America probably weren't either. Naps *were* on the list. God knew, Cooper needed one.

The scheduled mealtimes didn't work out quite right, either, but the junk food the three of them stuffed in their faces all day wouldn't show up on Ms. Perrell's list of acceptable meals anyway.

Cooper told himself he was too old, at

thirty-four, for stuff like this. In truth, he hadn't allowed himself such unbridled fun in years. He also suspected his two short co-conspirators knew exactly what they were up to, but they wouldn't rush to confess to their mom if it meant they'd be barred from more days like this. He hoped.

"It's about time we headed home, guys." Cooper valiantly attempted to wipe the worst of the ketchup off the kids' faces, groaning when they both simultaneously smeared half of it on their shirts and in their hair.

Ms. Perrell didn't say anything about laundry, did she? Cooper shuddered, unable to contemplate the thrills inherent in removing the stains these kids had acquired. He hoped they had lots of clean clothes. Knowing their mom, they must.

Emma and Alec, exhausted by the unexpected change from their daily routine, nonetheless murmured half-hearted protests. Seeing their eyelids drooping, Cooper saw through their mild whimpers but mentally saluted the effort. Herding them through the exit doors and out into the parking ramp, he found the midnight-blue SUV and lifted the couple little sacks of potatoes into their car seats. Out for the count. Cooper cranked up the classic rock station on the radio and, with blessed silence coming from the backseat, headed home.

Every telephone in the house was ringing as Cooper trundled in, a twin over each shoulder, a few minutes before five o'clock. After taking a moment to dump his load on the living-room couch, Cooper snagged the phone on the end table before the ringing stopped.

"Thank God you're there. I've been calling all afternoon. Are the kids okay? Did something happen? Is anything wrong?" Jarring his sleepy mood, the frantic tone threw him for a loop. Cooper waited for the woman to identify herself. She didn't, but at least the questions finally stopped.

"Can I ask who's calling? Is that you, Ms. Perrell? Why didn't you call my cell phone?" Grabbing his cell phone, Cooper quickly checked to make sure he hadn't missed any calls or texts. None. Whew. He figured whoever was calling now was either Molly Perrell, unable to stand the suspense of waiting until evening to check on her kids, or her sister-in-law, Nancy. But he wasn't about to answer these frantic questions in the dark.

"It's one Ms. Perrell, I guess, but call me

56

Nancy. Sorry for not identifying myself. I was too busy worrying about the kids. I assume this is Cooper Meredith?" Cooper heard her sigh in relief.

"Yeah, it's Cooper. The kids are fine, although currently sound asleep in an unsightly heap on the couch. We just got in the door when you called. Sorry I missed your calls earlier, but we had a busy day. They'll sleep for a while, I'd guess, but it'll be no trouble waking them up in time for you to get them at six."

Cooper wasn't sure about the hand-off arrangements, since the details of that had been included — he thought — in the barrage of information Ms. Perrell had peppered him with this morning. "Or did you want me to drop them off at your house? From what I remember, it's pretty close, isn't it?"

"Yes. Er, no. That is, that's why I've been trying to call you all afternoon, besides checking in to see how you're doing. What did you say you did all day?"

A warning buzzer was blaring in his head, but he couldn't figure out why. If Nancy lived a few blocks away, what could be the hassle in getting the kids to her? Either she'd pick them up, or he'd drive over to her house with them, and then come back and exchange the SUV for his convertible. Not a big deal either way.

He didn't have to be anywhere at any particular time, but Jake had mentioned getting together for a couple of beers at the end of Day One of Cooper's Grand Adventure.

Or what his mom kept calling his folly.

His teeth ground just thinking about it.

"I guess I didn't mention what we did all day. This and that. You know. Normal four-year-old stuff. Probably boring to mention. So, how did you want to handle my getting the kids to you? I guess it's only about an hour from now."

The day had been fun, but it needed to end. Soon. Which was worse — ten hours with these munchkins or ten hours in court? Come to think of it, ten hours in court didn't wear him out like this, and he could already feel himself about to go down for the count. He wouldn't complain if Nancy volunteered to take the kids early. First day on the job, she might feel sorry for him and do that.

"Well, I should probably come to the point. I've got a little problem, you see." As Nancy talked, the warning buzzer in Cooper's head became a crescendo of bells, sirens, and hammers, all threatening to split his skull.

Her next words magnified the threat. "Late this morning, I noticed these red spots on my little girl, Kelly, when I picked her up from her play group. And baby Charlie had a couple spots. I thought it was heat rash, but to be safe I called their doctor's office and was lucky enough to get them in to see her. That can be the toughest thing, seeing a doctor on short notice, don't you think?"

Get to the point. But I'm not going to like this. Cooper somehow knew the ending to the story but needed to hear it, word by painful word. He marveled at the similarities in Emma's and Nancy's methods of distracting him with endless gabbing.

Nancy might not be a blood relative to Emma, but Emma obviously spent far too much time with this woman. Actually, for someone about to dump on him big time, Nancy sounded like a nice person, someone he'd like. Less harried than her sister-in-law, that was for sure.

Not answering her somewhat rhetorical question, and opting instead for the silent treatment, Cooper let Nancy proceed to the ending he feared.

"Well, anyway, Dr. Monroe confirmed what I had been afraid of. Chicken pox.

With the spots Charlie already has, at least I don't need to worry about keeping him away from Kelly. And both of them will go through it at the same time, so I won't have to deal with this again. Unless Steve and I have more kids, but you never know, do you? Maybe one more. We haven't really given it much thought yet, you know?"

Cooper listened, his jaw dropping, as this woman he didn't know rattled on inanely. He was torn between dread of what he knew she would say and utter fascination with the meandering route she took to get there. Finally, he couldn't wait another minute.

"I'm sorry about your kids, Nancy, but what does this have to do with Alec and Emma? Is there a problem with you taking them tonight? If so, what does your sister-in-law want to do about it? Does she know? Are there other relatives in town, or should I look through her lists for the names of babysitters?"

"Actually, the thing is . . ." Nancy paused, then finally blurted out her inescapable conclusion. As she explained it, she had already considered and rejected all the possibilities, including those Cooper had rattled off and a host of others. No one was available. With each explanation, his spirits sank lower.

According to Nancy, she and Steve were Molly's only relatives in Minnesota, not counting the two or three weeks every summer that Steve and Molly's parents returned for a respite from the Sedona heat. Those weeks would come in August.

Nancy had called Molly's ex, Drew, earlier this afternoon. He'd already bailed out on his promise to take the kids while Molly was gone, but Nancy had tried him anyway. The guy had a date tonight and couldn't be bothered, even when reminded pointedly by Nancy of his DNA running around in the two children in question. *Loser.*

She'd also called all of Molly's babysitters, since they shared the same list. Of the few on the list old enough to handle overnight babysitting duties, none were available. The last of them had phoned her regrets twenty minutes ago. *Strike three.*

"I'm sorry, Cooper. I've tried. Anyone you could name, I've called. A couple of them, I even called back and begged. There's no one else who can do it. I'd send Steve, but he left town today, too, and I can't leave my kids or risk infecting Molly's. I know this is your first day on the job, but . . . well, I don't know what to say. I mean, you're there already, and it sounds like you've survived your first day with Alec and Emma, and, hey, aren't they great kids? It's such a nice change for Alec to have a guy around, even though Molly would sooner spit tacks than admit it. And Emma. What a doll. I mean, she can talk your ear off and all, but . . ."

Talk about the pot calling the kettle black. "So what you're saying is that I have to stay here with them? How long? I mean, just tonight, right? Can't someone else take over by tomorrow night? Does Molly know? Is she okay with it?"

She ought to be grateful, but he wouldn't bet on it. She'd probably be closer to petrified. She'd already turned her kids over to a stranger — a *male* stranger, no less — and now he was staying overnight with them.

He shook his head. He couldn't blame Molly for worrying, but Nancy was right: there wasn't any alternative short of catching the next flight home.

For him, staying overnight, when the kids would be in bed anyway, wouldn't be that much trouble. But, after doing the supreme favor for his new boss, he refused to take a hit for it.

"I haven't, um, called Molly yet, but if there's anything, anything at all, I can do to make this a one-night problem for you, of course I'd do it — I mean, I *will* do it. To be honest, though, since I ran down all my possibilities today without any luck, I'd hate to get your hopes up. The only other possibility is to call Molly in New York and have her come home. I hope it doesn't come to that, though, since the timing for her couldn't be worse."

Cooper wondered whether Nancy ever came up for air. Apparently not.

"Her boss, revenue pressures — well, I can't go into all the details, not right now, and it's probably not appropriate — although, really, I could go on and on all day about that boss of hers, the way he's been acting lately — but, no, I won't — anyway, no, I'd positively *hate* to have to call Molly right now. She doesn't know about this new wrinkle yet, because I'm still thinking about how to tell her. You don't happen to have any ideas, do you, Cooper? No, I know, I shouldn't involve you in my conversations with Molly. Well, I'll think of something."

Nancy trailed off into tangents that, thankfully, she didn't seem to feel the need to share with him. He finally realized that she'd hung up the phone without bringing the conversation to a conclusion and without so much as a goodbye.

Well, it wasn't his problem what she told Molly, unless of course it involved him taking the heat for something. Nancy didn't seem like that type of person, though, so his momentary worry managed to flit through his mind with only a brief stop. His only remaining thought was of the sharp contrast between Nancy and Molly. They were obviously close to each other, but to him as similar as oil and water.

After a quick call to Jake, still at the office, and a rain check for drinks another time, Cooper settled in for the evening ahead. Alec and Emma were still where he'd left them, a tangle of arms and legs on the couch. Cooper didn't have the energy to move them or, for that matter, to do much of anything at all.

What little energy he possessed was spent mulling the fantasy that the twins would magically fix their own dinner, amuse themselves until bedtime, and then go peacefully and very independently off to bed at some early hour. Like, maybe, six-thirty.

He'd have to grab some clothes and his shaving kit from the condo, but that could wait until tomorrow. Tonight, his body wasn't going anywhere.

Having dozed off in a chair by the couch, Cooper awakened to find two miniature human pretzels attached to his legs, each with a grip of steel. A grip he was growing accustomed to, having experienced it upon the dynamic duo's first attack yesterday afternoon, and repeatedly and indiscriminately this afternoon on every ride offered at Nickelodeon Universe.

At the moment, the little blond bookends appeared to be clinging by unspoken agreement, as their pose and grip weren't accompanied by the usual whine, buzz, screech, or roar but, instead, by blissful silence.

For once, Alec broke the silence. "Cooper! Cooper! What are we gonna do now, Cooper?"

Alec wasn't the only twin feeling oh-so-cool to be able to use Cooper's first name, but he'd used it so much all day that Cooper seriously considered returning to those initial moments with the ever-changing permutations of "Mr. Meredith." Either that, or Alec would eventually wear out or discover that Cooper's name wasn't, in fact, the "coolest" name he'd ever heard.

About the same time he'll stop staring at me with that hero worship in those innocent eyes, Cooper thought, gazing at the pretzel attached to his right leg. He mentally disavowed all notions of being anyone's hero or role model. He had to admit, though, it wasn't the worst thing in the world. From where he sat, and even with a couple of sticky pretzels attached to him, Cooper felt a lot better than he had in a long, long time.

Tapping her toes, her gaze skittering ceaselessly between her appointment book, her watch, and a room full of critical business contacts, Molly waited for someone, *anyone,* to pick up the phone at Nancy's. No answer all evening, and no answer on Nancy's cell phone to any of Molly's half-million calls and texts. Steve and Nancy had caller ID and sometimes used it to screen out solicitors, but Molly's name and cell phone number on the screen would let them know to pick up.

Finally, out of desperation, Molly called her own number at home. Alec answered on the third ring. With his childlike "hello" still floating into the receiver, Molly was torn between relief and sheer terror.

What on earth had happened? Were Emma and Alec safe?

"Let me talk to Aunt Nancy, sweetie." Molly didn't want to scare Alec, but she wanted some answers. Fast.

"Aunt Nancy's not here, Mommy. Do you want to talk to Cooper? He's making us peanut butter sammiches, though, and I bet his hands are kinda sticky. Mine are pretty clean, though, so you could talk to me."

"Cooper? I mean, Mr. Meredith? You should call him Mr. Meredith, Alec. Please ask Mr. Meredith to clean his hands, if he needs to, and to pick up the phone."

"Okay, Mommy, I'll tell him. But he said we can call him Cooper, 'cause Emma couldn't say his name, and 'cause we're pretty big kids and all. But I'll tell him you said to wash his hands."

"That's not quite what I —" Hearing the phone crash against the kitchen floor, Molly decided to save her breath, especially since she suspected she'd need all of her wind to handle what she feared would be an ugly conversation with Cooper Meredith.

"Hi, Ms. Perrell. The hands are sparkling clean, I'm pleased to report. What can I do for you?"

Molly nearly trembled with the anxiety that had built all evening, even though the rational part of her assured her that the kids were okay. Not on schedule, probably not even remotely under control, but alive, well, and . . . okay. That assurance didn't stop the stream of questions that flew out of her mouth.

"*What* has happened, *where* is Nancy, and for God's sake *why* are you still with my children?"

Chapter Four

It was too late to claim she'd called a wrong number. Hanging up on her, maybe even loudly, had its merits but was a short-term solution. Knowing her, Ms. Perrell's next call might be to the police. *Just a little joke, Molly,* probably wouldn't suffice as an excuse, either to her or to the uniform waiting to slap a pair of handcuffs on him.

Faking a seizure, even if it produced more of those high-pitched giggles out of the twins, was starting to look appealing to Cooper when a soft "Please tell me everything's okay" on the other end of the line brought him out of his daze and reminded him it was time to face down his opponent.

That's right, Cooper reflected as he tried to focus on the best responses to the interrogatories she'd flung at him. *She's just another opponent. Pretend you're in court with her. You can win this.*

Reminding himself that Molly Perrell was

the one with the problem that *he* was fixing, Cooper summoned up a vision of his old senior partner, Tom Garrison. No one was as bad as Garrison, but when Molly Perrell was terrified about her kids, she gave him a run for his money. Hell, she could almost out-Garrison Garrison. On his worst day.

He touched a hand to his head — which was sticky, he realized, thanks to one or both of the kids — and reminded himself that Molly wasn't really his opponent. She *was* terrified about her kids, and she had a right to be. Garrison had never had that excuse.

"I take it you haven't talked to Nancy?" Cooper opted for a safe, calm, nondefensive approach. Besides, it might give him a little info, or at least buy him time to come up with a decent response.

"*No,* I haven't talked to Nancy, as you probably know. What happened to her? Didn't you call her? And what's going on with my kids? Are they okay? Unless you give me a good answer in the next thirty seconds, I'm catching the next flight out of here."

Something in the back of her mind told Molly she was being unreasonable, unfair, and a dozen other things she'd regret in the morning. Too late. She already did. But the awful fears and self-doubts she'd gone through — not knowing what was happening to her kids, not absolutely sure she hadn't left them with an ax-murderer — left her ready to commit murder herself. And Cooper Meredith was the handiest target in sight.

She blew out a calming breath. She'd already talked to Alec. Her kids were okay.

She hoped.

"Nancy's kids both have chicken pox." He sounded so calm. So sure of himself. So unlike Molly at the moment. "She discovered it around noon today and asked me to stay overnight here. Nancy obviously couldn't come, her husband is out of town, and she couldn't have your kids stay at her house, or all four kids would have chicken pox. So here I am. Nancy said I'd have to stay the rest of the week, too, until you get back, because no one else can, and I guess her kids will still be contagious. So there's your thirty-second answer. Any rebuttal?"

Molly winced at that last jab. She deserved it. Aware that she should be grateful for his last-minute help — and she was — she sure hadn't sounded like it. Instead, she'd practically accused him of murder, or worse. But she was a thousand miles away and felt . . .

70

helpless.

Though his words to her were short, almost clipped, his wasn't the voice of an ax-murderer. It was more of a scotch-on-the-rocks voice, flowing through the telephone, taking her mind meandering through all sorts of warm, fuzzy stirrings before letting it land on one delicious thought. Or more than one. Each of which she promptly discarded.

Forget the voice, she commanded herself. Irritated, she ran a hand through her hair, her fingers getting caught on a tangle. The week was far from over, and she had to get herself and her kids through it.

Molly forced herself to count to ten . . . slowly, knowing she had to bring herself under control. She reminded herself that even with this latest minor catastrophe, Cooper Meredith didn't appear anywhere close to being in the running with her last nanny — the one eager to demonstrate the latest and greatest waterboarding techniques to four-year-olds. That calmed her. And after all, Cooper wasn't the problem. He was the solution. Maybe her twice-a-week yoga classes were paying off. Either that, or she'd reached a new level of desperation when it came to nannies.

"Thank God you don't seem like the

waterboarding type, Cooper," she finally said, knowing her faint praise would be lost on him.

Realizing that his failure to respond might mean he wasn't following her train of thought — thankfully — Molly gave a belated and somewhat half-hearted chuckle. It came out more like the gurgle of a drowning woman, or maybe a hacking cough. She suspected the laugh track inside her had simply dried up from lack of use.

Cooper. She finally dropped the "Mr. Meredith" nonsense and, for a moment, let herself relax. Did he even notice? Or care? Probably not. But she was tired, and all the emotional armor she wore weighed more than she could handle right now.

"Look, Molly — hey, is it okay if I call you Molly?" Cooper didn't wait for a response. Just as well. "I realize this trip to New York is crucial to your job. Trust me, I understand those kinds of work demands. The kids are fine. Great, in fact. We got a little behind schedule, but otherwise we're right on track, and it's no big problem for me to stay here until you get back on Thursday. Thursday, right? No problem at all."

Molly wished that were the case. She'd really counted on Nancy. Cooper was making her children peanut butter sandwiches instead of the balanced dinner she always insisted on and regarding which she had given Cooper precise instructions. And her watch told her that these very same peanut butter sandwiches were being eaten at nine o'clock at night — one hour past Alec's and Emma's absolute bedtime and a whopping three hours past their dinnertime.

She tried not to groan. She really did.

"Uh . . . why, exactly, are the children having dinner at nine o'clock at night? And why are they eating peanut butter sandwiches, if I might ask?"

Molly didn't really want to hear the answer, but calmer now, she was trying to figure out how bad the situation was, and how short she had to cut her trip. She needed to be in New York and was scheduled nonstop with designers, sales reps, and advertisers until noon on Thursday. Every cell in her body wanted to quit, come home, and be with her children. But she couldn't. For once, couldn't everything somehow manage to go her way?

Cooper cleared his throat. A couple times. This couldn't be good. "With the confusion over everything happening at Nancy's house and all, and with lunch having been so filling for Emma and Alec, we got started a bit late on dinner. Since I realized that adhering to the bedtime schedule was important, I thought that peanut butter sandwiches would be both speedy and nutritious. Especially . . ."

He paused, and Molly forced herself to ignore the frantic rattles and bangs of cupboards and the refrigerator being opened and closed as he spoke. She tried not to analyze what it meant.

"Especially?" As the pause lengthened, Molly waited to hear what came next. Wisely, she chose not to ask why lunch had been so "filling."

"Oh, yeah." The creaky cupboard over the sink opened, then closed. "As I was saying, especially when I put the sandwiches together with carrots and fresh strawberries." Which, if she had to guess, he then started to do. Right that moment.

"I guess that sounds okay." It didn't sound all that great to Molly, but Alec and Emma also wouldn't die of malnutrition. Not before Thursday.

"Great. Well, the kids should start getting ready for bed about now, so I should probably sign off . . ."

She sensed his impatience. Was she that awful to talk to? Her relief at the children's safety and desire for them to get to sleep close to their normal bedtime warred with her desire to find out more about what had happened today. Exhausted by her flight and the frenetic rounds of meetings, which had just ended, she decided to postpone any further questions until she was refreshed, alert, and up to the challenge. At the moment, she'd settle for two out of three.

"I suppose you're right. And, by the way, yes, please call me Molly. I should've said that sooner. I'll let you go now, but I really do appreciate you coming to the rescue like this. Thanks." She tried not to imagine what would've happened if Cooper *hadn't* been able or willing to stay overnight. She owed him. No matter what he fed the kids at nine p.m. "I'll check in as soon as I can tomorrow, and I'll check on the possibility of coming home sooner than Thursday afternoon."

Barring an emergency, the odds of being able to move up her departure were extremely low. And even she couldn't call peanut butter sandwiches at nine o'clock at night an emergency.

"Whatever works."

Whatever works? Something else not to think about. "In the meantime, please call me immediately if anything happens. And, please, I'd really like it if the children got back on schedule tomorrow. Just read the

instructions I left for you. Maybe after settling in with them for a day, you'll find the
schedule much easier to keep."

"Yeah. Sure."

And maybe pigs will fly. She doubted he'd
even try. Just before she hit the "off" button
on the phone, she heard an audible sigh of
relief from Cooper. From the sound of it,
he had his work cut out for him.

The next morning, and afternoon and
evening, brought no relief to the frenzied
chaos of Molly's life. Hassles with suppliers
over timing and availability of orders. Arguments with designers over last-minute,
drastic changes in the fall shows and just-
announced cancellations of several segments
of next season's lines. Bafflement over all
the new names and faces, just when it
seemed that she'd gotten to know — and
gotten "in" with — the big-name contacts
in the industry.

And what was going on with her boss, Jed
Parker? He was practically invisible at the
meetings, at a time when his connections
and his position at Harrowby's could have
smoothed the way for Molly over the minor
speed bumps she kept hitting in New York.
In the few snatches of time she'd grabbed
with Jed — stray moments in the hallway,

lobby, or elevator — he'd seemed pre-occupied or, more often, engrossed in conversation with what looked to be a college intern.

Once, distracted by something Molly said to him, Jed had absentmindedly introduced her to the intern. Susie something-or-other. Susie had blushed and tittered, fanning her face with two-inch nails, brushing back her cascading auburn curls, and bobbing and weaving on five-inch platform heels while wearing a spandex miniskirt. *Makes quite an impression,* Molly thought, but didn't think much beyond that. She had far more on her mind.

Mumbling her apologies for dashing off and not waiting for a response from Jed and Susie, neither of whom appeared to notice her leave, Molly headed up to the fourteenth floor, where the key designers and their sales reps had booked several suites of rooms.

When Molly's tenacious assistant finagled a critical last-minute meeting with the notoriously in-demand sales rep for Jacques Rives, the current hot designer for twenty-somethings whose apparel was flying off the racks, Molly couldn't pass it up. She valued her life too much. And Jed Parker — not to mention her assistant, Greta Marshall —

would certainly have killed her. On the other hand, the only time the sales rep had available was the half hour Molly had squirreled away for herself for lunch, a sanity break, and phone calls home.

She needed a break. In more ways than one.

Exuberant from her success in nailing a sizable shipment of the Jacques Rives winter line, but too wiped out to care, Molly choked down a trail bar with an Evian chaser, prayed that none of it landed on her blouse, and dashed to a quiet room before the buyers' conference at two o'clock. Running the meeting for the first time, it would be her high-profile moment of the week, and she couldn't blow it. As she checked her watch for the hundredth time that day, Molly saw she had exactly three minutes left to fix any problems at home. No sweat. Ha.

As she let the phone ring what seemed like twenty times, Molly wondered, with growing concern, where Nancy could be. No answer on either of Nancy's phones, and even voice mail didn't pick up. She'd have to ask Cooper to check on Nancy. But how could he do that without leaving Alec and Emma on their own, or exposing them to

Nancy's kids? Worse, what if Cooper had fed the twins so much peanut butter, all three of them were permanently rolled into round balls by now and stuck to the furniture?

Yeah, and why don't you go back to the waterboarding scenario while you're at it, she thought with a laugh. The lack of sleep and overabundance of catastrophes were catching up with her. She'd turned into a crazed lunatic. Perfect.

Realizing how ludicrous her imaginings had become, Molly shook her head, straightened her shoulders, and headed into the buyers' conference with a confident gleam plastered on her face. If she could get through this, she'd have time in a couple hours to focus on things at home. That would have to be good enough. The kids, and Nancy, and Cooper, were undoubtedly fine.

The kids were more than fine. By their standards, at least, and even by Cooper's — such as they were — but undoubtedly not by Molly's. If he hadn't known that intuitively, Cooper realized it in a hurry when he finally hunted down the long-ignored instructions from Molly.

The crumpled-up, chewed-on sheets of

instructions now included, on top of the words penned in Molly's precise handwriting, peanut butter stains, muddy footprints, juice splashes, a very squashed and formerly juicy bug of indeterminate species, and a few other stains the origin of which Cooper didn't want to spend much time exploring.

By three-thirty that afternoon, Cooper quit wondering when Molly might call with more questions to follow up on last night's. No point worrying about something he couldn't control, which was an understatement when it came to these miniature hoodlums.

Another glance at his cell phone and Molly's caller ID confirmed that she hadn't even made an attempt. Good thing, he figured, as he paused a moment during a quick trip into the house from the tree house "club" — to which he had, after some serious consideration by the two small ruling members of the club, been admitted. He was a probationary member only, of course, as Emma had solemnly informed him. Well, as solemnly as she could, having ventured even more iterations of the word "probationary" and its cousins than she had of "Meredith" the day before. She'd finally given up with a shrug, a wagging finger, and a "you know what I mean."

Dawn broke early in the Perrell household. With it, so did a crystal wineglass that only recently had been cupped in Emma's chubby little hands and filled with grape juice helpfully poured by Alec. Or the other way around. Cooper couldn't get the story straight from the two accomplices in short pants. The day didn't improve much from its dramatic opening, at least from the perspective of someone who liked organization, structure, and routine. Like Molly. Cooper was adapting, though.

With great ease, the twins were also adapting: to a strategy of intentionally confusing him, which was working with remarkable success. Seldom beaten in court, on only his second day with these two, Cooper was outmanned and outgunned.

"Cooper! Cooper! Look what we found!" Something that looked dead, hairy, and disgusting even to Cooper was dangling from Alec's outstretched fingers, as his little legs dangled precariously from a branch that supported the tree house.

As Cooper rushed to the tree to catch Alec before the inevitable fall and resulting concussion, he glimpsed someone approaching from the house next door. After barely averting yet another self-imposed and potentially fatal injury to Alec, Cooper took a deep breath — at least his fortieth today required by Alec's and Emma's adventures — and promptly choked on it. The "someone" from next door appeared to have forgotten most of her clothes.

"Hel-loooo, handsome! What brings you to poor little Molly's house, and whatever insignificant thing could be keeping you away from mine?" Grinning wickedly, the woman looked as if she were examining the various parts of his anatomy in intimate detail. Cooper was grateful not to be privy to the woman's thoughts, but he couldn't avoid noticing what the woman had on. Or what she didn't.

A barely-there thong bikini that, probably not accidentally, happened to be the same color as her cocoa-brown tan, appeared to be glued to a few strategic specks of skin. Two of the scraps of fabric were clearly intended to focus his gaze on a set of boobs a lot like the ones in the Penthouse subscription Cooper handed off to his little brother when he left for college. He'd bet good money that, like most of the Penthouse boobs, these were fake, too. A sheer gauze skirt approximately the size of a Band-Aid, neon pink nails on both hands and feet, Ray-Ban sunglasses, and streaked, hairsprayed mahogany tresses completed the picture.

Or, Cooper figured, overexposed it.

Though caught off guard and indifferent but not blind to the wares she was offering, Cooper mentally shook his head at the spectacle. The buxom brunette from next door had plenty of gall to match her over-the-top looks. As she bounced ever closer to Cooper, ready to pounce, Cooper wondered if she could get dressed and help babysit. This was what it had come to: checking out hot women only for their potential to make PB and J sandwiches.

With the neighbor now almost upon him — literally, he feared — Cooper fixed a smile on his face. "Hi. Cooper Meredith. I'm taking care of Emma and Alec. The new, you know, nanny." He was still adjusting to calling himself that. Although he didn't much care about this woman's opinion of him, he still asked himself why he was playing babysitter, and whether he hadn't lost his marbles.

"Oh. Right." With a conspiratorial wink and artificial chuckle, she cozied up a little closer to him. If that were possible. "No, really — why are you playing with the kids? Relative of Molly's? Where is that girl, anyway?"

Cooper felt himself grow irritated, but his smile remained firmly in place. For now. "No, really. I'm the new nanny. Just started yesterday, and Molly's out of town on business. And you are — ?"

The neighbor drew herself up straighter, managing in the process to flaunt every curve she had. As she licked her lips, a feral gleam came into her eyes. She was either sizing him up or deciding which barbecue sauce she'd marinate him in. He fought an urge to make sure he was still wearing clothes, or if her eyes had successfully removed them.

"Oh, my. You're serious. I never . . . well, that's so *interesting*. I guess that makes us practically neighbors. How delightful. Oh, yes — I'm Brooke Fieldstone. So Molly hasn't mentioned me? Well, I'm sure we'll have no trouble getting acquainted."

Brooke was clearly stunned by the news of his employment but gamely willing to proceed. On any basis, as far as Cooper could tell.

She wouldn't be making more moves anytime soon, though. Emma was tired of being ignored and, as far as Cooper could tell when he glanced down at her, didn't want her new friend playing with Brooke instead of her. With brow furrowed, tongue planted firmly between her teeth, and hands on her nonexistent hips, she gave her best impression of a drill sergeant and started barking orders. Or, at least, squeaking them.

"Cooper! Mommy said we should go inside now. Isn't it quarter after two-thirty? I think so. We're supposed to have Kool-Aid and lots of cookies. That's what Mommy wants, I know she does. She told me so. So can we, huh, can we, Cooper? Now? Plee-ease?"

Cooper very much doubted that Molly kept any Kool-Aid in the house or would ever let Kool-Aid slide down the throats of these two kids. The cookies weren't on the instruction list, either. Emma had given him an easy out with Brooke, though, and for that he was grateful. Grateful enough to dig up some Kool-Aid and cookies for Emma and her little comrade-in-arms, Alec.

"Sorry, Brooke, I guess it's snack time. Gotta go, you know? Good to meet you. I'm sure we'll see you around. Thanks for stopping by." As Brooke gave him one last salacious look, nearly skewering him, Cooper whirled and practically ran into the house. Safe at last.

Molly, with relief but weary impatience,

basked in the admiring praise of the last of the stragglers coming out of the three-hour buyers' conference. *Ten after five,* she saw as she sneaked a surreptitious glance at her watch while mumbling her thanks to the key organizer of the event. Wilted, and famished from skipping lunch, she shifted in place on aching feet. On the brink of collapse, she remembered that she could skip this evening's scheduled cocktail hour, so she could put up her blistering feet for an hour or so before the "impromptu" dinner at six-thirty with forty colleagues in the industry.

Before she could relax, though, she had to find out what was going on at home. Ten minutes later, in her hotel suite, Molly temporarily set aside her concerns about Nancy and dialed her own home. Catching Cooper on the second ring, she breathed a sigh of relief.

"Cooper! Thank God. I haven't been able to reach Nancy all day and was almost beginning to wonder if someone had blown Minneapolis off the map today."

"All present and accounted for, ma'am, with all body parts safely intact."

Still dazed from her whirlwind day and saving her focus for the long evening ahead, Molly glossed over any thought of body parts, Cooper's or otherwise. She wanted only to make sure her kids were safe and, somehow, if she could, find out what had happened to Nancy. She had no energy left at the moment for anything beyond that.

"Listen, Cooper, I haven't had any chance yet to see whether I can change my schedule for this week, but I'm not optimistic. How are Emma and Alec? Have you heard from Nancy today? What's happening with her?" Shrugging out of her suit jacket while she waited expectantly for his response, Molly sank onto the couch in her hotel suite and leaned back against the cushions.

"No problems here. We've had a great day, and both kids are napping now. I haven't heard from Nancy, but I didn't really expect to, so . . ." Cooper trailed off. He obviously had no idea what was up with Nancy. Nancy must be as incommunicado with him as she was being with Molly.

With a calm conviction that what she didn't know might not hurt her, Molly decided to spare Cooper the third degree about the kids' day. She might find out more than she could handle right now, and she didn't have a lot of options for the next couple days. Deciding that a constant stream of prayers would have to suffice, she pursued the Nancy question.

"I tried to reach Nancy all evening yesterday, with no success. I haven't had more than a few free moments today, but I called her every chance I could. If Kelly and Charlie are both sick, she must be at home. She has to be. Unless something awful happened. I can't imagine what it can be, and I'm starting to get worried."

Absorbed in her concerns about her brother Steve's family, Molly forgot for a moment her own doubts about Cooper and his childcare skills as she let Cooper glimpse past her stoic façade and shared her growing panic about Nancy. In doing so, she felt herself open a window, at least by a crack, into her interior. Amazing, really. She seldom let that happen. She couldn't afford to.

"Look, Molly, I'm sure it's nothing. If it makes you feel better, though, I'll call Nancy myself and, if that doesn't work, I'll hop in the car with the kids and drive over to her house."

"But —"

"And before you start worrying about something else, I've already had chicken pox, and I'll leave Alec and Emma in the car so they don't get exposed. And, no, I won't let them out of my sight. I'll stand on the front steps and talk to her from there."

Despite knowing her for only a couple of days, Cooper somehow guessed at the questions, and follow-up questions, she would've had for him and flooded her with more details than anyone other than Molly would want to know.

She loved it. She'd been torn between a burning desire to make sure Nancy was okay and her all-out concern that her own kids not get sick or harmed while Cooper checked on Nancy. Drew would never have thought it through as Cooper had, instead always leaving Molly to shoulder both the worries and the solutions.

Without letting herself analyze why she was comparing Cooper to Drew, let alone why she found the low rumble of Cooper's voice so ridiculously soothing, Molly felt a moment's contentment. For once, it wasn't all hers to handle. Finishing the phone call with a few minutes of idle chatter, she stretched out on the couch. And smiled.

CHAPTER FIVE

Day three of nannyville. No broken crystal today — yet. No broken bones — yet. All in all, a remarkable success. With no one around to challenge that assessment, Cooper felt pretty darned smug about the whole thing. And here it was, already ten o'clock in the morning. The day was practically gone!

Chuckling to himself, Cooper decided this was turning out to be an okay gig after all. He wondered in passing who Molly hired to do the laundry, clean up the house, stuff like that, but chose not to focus too rigidly on Molly's written instructions, which mysteriously skipped from page two to page four. Molly was probably off on her page numbering. Whatever the case, Cooper *knew* the instructions couldn't include anything more than taking care of the kids.

Although . . . Emma and Alec tracked an amazing amount of dirt onto the white living-room carpet. And how did two little kids manage to wear, and completely destroy, so many clothes? And the dishes were definitely starting to pile up in the sink. Where would Molly have hidden the paper plates, anyway?

"Cooper!"

Emma's shrill little squeal still hanging in the air, Cooper winced, then peered around the morning paper at the pint-sized cutie in a yellow striped top and pink polka-dot shorts. "Yeah, Emma? What's up, doll?"

"Cooper," she began, "wouldn't it be lots and lots of fun to go swimming? We'd be extra super careful, and Mommy likes us to swim, and I'm a big girl and can swim real good. Alec's good, too, but he's a big boy. He's not a big girl."

Thanking her for the helpful distinction, Cooper tried to discern what Emma really wanted and why Molly would absolutely object to it. They'd gone to Lake Harriet on Monday, even though the munchkins just waded in up to their thighs before squealing and running back onto the sand.

So what was the big deal this time?

Emma, always spilling happy chatter around the room, gushed even more enthusiastically when she set her sights on something objectionable. Cooper had figured that out almost immediately. Emma's poker face was good, but Cooper was a few years and countless Friday-night poker games ahead of her. When Alec was in the same room, Cooper was better at figuring out Emma's little plots, since Alec's impulse to turn red at each attempted transgression gave his sister away every time.

With Alec nowhere in sight, Cooper was on his own.

"Cooper?" Rattling both his hand and the newspaper still attached to it, Emma looked at him with luminous eyes, clearly torn between sending him a pleading look and batting those tiny eyelashes. Opting for something in between, she wound up looking at him somehow cross-eyed.

Undaunted by his silence, the little blond pixie plunged ahead. "Is it okay, Cooper? Pleeeease? Mommy said so. Yes, she said so at least twelve-teen times before she flew away on the big plane. I'll put on my swimsuit. Don't worry, I'm a big girl. I can find it. Thanks, Cooper!"

Tripping happily down the hall to the first door on the left, Emma slammed the door before squealing with victorious delight. Still unable to figure out what the miniature criminal mastermind could be up to, Cooper put down the paper, ran a hand through his hair, and stood up. Time to find Alec. If Emma had something up her sleeve, he wanted to keep an eye on her cohort as well.

Ten minutes later, with Alec retrieved from his hiding place inside the clothes dryer, both Cooper and Alec were in swimsuits and waiting in the shallow end of Molly's backyard pool for Emma to appear. Appear she did. In a little yellow-and-blue striped two-piece, an enormous pair of brown flip-flops on her feet, and a pair of Molly's red designer sunglasses with the price tag still on. Emma had also raided Molly's makeup case, finishing her look with a bold dash of coral lipstick. On her lips and halfway across her cheek.

After splashing in the pool for an hour, Cooper realized that Emma had nothing more diabolical in mind than putting on a fashion show — such as it was — in the absence of Molly. Sure, Molly might shriek in an uncanny imitation of her daughter if she were here.

But she wasn't here. He was.

Toweling off, then turning to cajole Alec and Emma out of the pool and help them dry off, Cooper glanced over the backyard fence and into Brooke Fieldstone's backyard. And nearly dropped his towel as well as his teeth. There, lying in a chaise lounge next to her own swimming pool, was the very topless Brooke. Waving at him.

Too late to pretend he hadn't seen her, Cooper looked down at the kids, who were absorbed in getting the last splashes out of the pool and trying without success to snap their towels at each other. No direct towel hits resulted, but they inadvertently dried themselves with the mild breeze they generated. Whatever worked.

Relieved that the kids didn't notice Brooke, Cooper shook his head, tired of the woman's misdirected antics and wondering whether she did this all the time, or only for his benefit. He figured some of both. Wanting only to escape, Cooper aimed a careless wave in Brooke's direction, looked everywhere but at her, and walked back into the house.

". . . and old man Garrison thought the man in the mirror was the thief, so he conked himself on the head, tripped down the stairs, rolled out the front door to the street, was swept into the river by the street sweeper, and floated away, never to be heard from again. And everybody else lived happily ever after. The end. Now, nap time, you two." Relieved to come up with a slam-bang finish to his latest impromptu story for the kids, Cooper leaned back on the end of Alec's bed, against the wall.

"I don't believe it! Mr. Garrison couldn't be that dopey, could he?" Alec exclaimed.

"If Cooper says so, it must be so," declared Cooper's fan, Emma.

"No, it's not!"

"It is too!"

"You're wrong, you're wrong! He's making it up. At least, I think so. Isn't that true, Cooper? Isn't it?" Alec's self-confidence waned more with each word he spoke. Cooper would have to work with him on that, or he was doomed to lose every war of words to his sister.

"Well, you know, guys, it's generally true except when it's not. So, you might be right or wrong depending on how you look at it, and, for what it's worth, old man Garrison isn't a pretty sight to look at, you know? So, in a sense, you're both right. This time." Cooper knew, from the glazed and befuddled looks on their faces, that his legal mumbo jumbo had confused them enough to stop a fight before it blazed out of control.

"Oh . . . okay," Alec and Emma said, almost in unison.

"And, besides, I see right through you, you diabolical monsters. Ha! It's nap time, and you're cleverly trying to distract me.

Well, you're not clever enough to fool the mighty Meredith. Clearly, I must punish you for this wicked deed." Cooper paused for effect. "I'll be forced to . . . tickle you!"

High-pitched squealing assaulted Cooper's ears. His eyes beheld Alec's chubby little legs flailing to escape underneath the covers, while Emma raced across the hall to her room and slammed the door, giggling and out of breath.

Smiling, Cooper ambled into the living room, retrieved the book he hadn't touched since arriving Monday, and turned to page five. And promptly fell asleep.

Fifteen minutes later, the shrill ringing of the phone on the end table next to him jarred Cooper out of a sound sleep. Glancing at his watch — a habit from his law firm years that would die hard — Cooper hoped the kids wouldn't wake up. Their naps were more critical to his well-being than to theirs.

As he mumbled a sleep-induced, husky greeting into the phone, Cooper suddenly remembered his promise to Molly. He'd forgotten to call or check on Nancy. With any luck, Molly wasn't calling, and he could still find Nancy and successfully report in to Molly.

Wrong. Molly. Maybe this wasn't his day, after all.

■ ■ ■ ■

"Cooper? Hi. I had a quick break between meetings and thought I'd check on Alec and Emma. And I'm still worried about Nancy. What did you find out?"

Realizing her shoulders were hunched from stress, maybe permanently, Molly tried to bend her neck in every direction. She nearly dropped the phone.

"To tell the truth, Molly, I haven't had any luck finding Nancy yet."

She hoped Nancy was all right. Well, at least she could hear about Alec and Emma. Before she could ask anything, Cooper continued. "The kids have had a hectic but good day, though, and are taking their naps now. We swam in the pool, told some stories, you know, the stuff on your list."

"Oh." Molly's brain was still somewhat addled from lack of sleep and too many people shouting too many things at her, usually all at once. What little was left of her mind was tracing over the soft, barely-there "Hello" that greeted her when Cooper had picked up the phone. His was a voice a woman ached to wake up to, hinting at pleasures she'd long since forgotten. *Where did that come from, Moll?* she asked herself, shaking her head in a fruitless attempt to clear it of unwanted thoughts about her nanny.

Attributing her stray musings to lack of sleep, Molly brushed them off. Back to Cooper. Her nanny, not her . . . anything else.

"Well. Yes." She was having some difficulty functioning or following simple commands. Like, say, forcing her tongue to speak.

Cooper broke the silence. "What's up with you, Molly? Everything going great? Still coming home tomorrow afternoon, or were you able to book an earlier flight?"

"Oh, right. I forgot to tell you. Things are hectic here but going pretty well. Except with my boss, who's been a bit strange on this trip, but . . . well, that's probably nothing worth mentioning. I don't think you know him." Jed Parker. Molly thought about his increasingly bizarre behavior over the last couple days.

The intern, or whatever she was, practically clung to him, hanging on his every word. Susie Dixon. The name didn't ring a bell, and Molly was usually involved in every hiring decision in the buying group at Harrowby's. She'd have to ask Greta about it when she got back in the office. Jed normally couldn't be bothered to listen to the endless prattle of the execs at his level or Molly's, let alone spare a moment for a young kid like Susie.

If it were anyone but Jed, Molly would almost wonder if something was going on between the two. She easily dismissed it. Jed always bragged about his perfect wife and perfect kids, who were now in college or getting ready for it, having received — if Jed could be believed — every award or honor ever handed out. They probably won the Pulitzer last week.

Besides, Molly thought with a rare smirk, the guy had a handshake like a dead fish, and his breath wasn't too far from that. She'd never heard any woman at work utter a word about him that wasn't related to work, and *that* had to be a new world record for the women she worked with. So, no, she couldn't explain his recent preoccupation with this Susie. A niece? She'd have to check it out.

Remembering Cooper on the other end of the line, she reined in her train of thought. "Anyway, everything else is great. At least, great if sleep isn't a big priority. I could sleep a week." *With you.*

Where had *that* thought come from? She didn't even know the guy. It was maybe just something about his voice. On his answering machine, on the phone.

She shook her head, glad the phone prevented him from seeing the blush stealing over her cheeks. "Anyway. I have a big meeting tonight, so I can't make it out of here today. My travel coordinator worked wonders, though, and somehow got me on the eight-thirty flight out of here in the morning, which was sold out. I should make it back to the house by eleven or so tomorrow morning and can take the rest of the day off."

"That sounds great. Maybe you can catch up on some rest. I know the kids can't wait to see you."

Part of her hoped *he* couldn't wait to see her, either, but she couldn't expect a miracle. They hadn't begun well. Every phone call between them, though, had been further relaxed, piquing her interest. She wondered if they'd do as well in person.

"Thanks, Cooper. Give them my love, and tell them I can't wait to hug and kiss my . . . my little bunnies to death when I see them tomorrow. I've got to run. Talk to you later." Startling herself by letting slip to Cooper words she used only in front of Emma and Alec, Molly raced to get off the phone. *Ugh.* The trip must be getting to her. She was starting to embarrass herself. That had to stop.

Blinking, Cooper slowly replaced the phone on the receiver. *My little bunnies?* Had the woman had a lobotomy in New York? Molly sounded almost . . . cute.

Moments later, a call to Nancy unraveled the ongoing mystery. Answering on the first ring, her breathless "Hello? Cooper?" startled him as he plotted the process of driving over to her house with Emma and Alec in tow.

"Nancy? What's going on? Molly says she's been trying to reach you since Monday and hasn't been able to. Is something wrong? You should've called. Maybe I could've helped."

As he quizzed her, Cooper wondered whether it could've been as simple as Molly punching the wrong name or number into her phone. Molly didn't seem like the type to make a mistake like that, and certainly not to repeat it, but maybe New York was stressing her too much. She wouldn't be the first to succumb to that.

No. Impossible. Nancy's name and numbers would be in Molly's cell phone. She couldn't misdial. It had to be something on Nancy's end.

"Oh, Cooper, everything's fine. Kelly and Charlie both look like one huge spot right now, and they're driving me nuts with all that itching and complaining, but we're managing. It seems like it's been three weeks, not just three days, what with all the running around to get this or that for them. Steve arrived back in town today, which helps a lot. Yes, we're getting by. But thanks for offering. That's awfully sweet."

Nancy didn't say why she'd missed all those phone calls Molly had made to Nancy. Glad to hear there was no real issue, Cooper voiced his suspicion. "I'm glad everything's working out, Nancy, but what about Molly trying to reach you? Do you think she might have misdialed?"

Even though it was basically impossible.

Nancy sucked in her breath. Audibly. "No, I can't imagine she did. Molly just . . . well, she doesn't make mistakes like that, like someone else might. Even when she's rushed. She's the most organized person I know. Maybe the most organized person in the whole world — doesn't it seem that way? But, speaking of rushed, I'll bet she's pretty rushed right now in New York. Twice a year she has to make that trip, and, I swear, each time it's crazier than the last. You must've had trips like that when you worked for a law firm, huh?"

After three days with Emma and only a couple of mind-numbing telephone conversations like this with Nancy, Cooper asked himself how those two could be related only by marriage, and not by blood. Their ability to shift from subject to subject, without regard for logic or linear thought processes, unnerved him. Getting a straight answer out of either of them was next to impossible.

"Uh, Nancy, I don't mean to interrupt, but I really am wondering what's up. Do you have any idea why Molly couldn't reach you? She keeps asking me every time she calls, and I don't know what to say."

"Oh. Well, I suppose I've put you in a tough position. I hadn't thought about that. I'm sorry. I . . . well, I . . . it's just that . . . well, you know Molly . . ." Obviously nervous, Nancy began to stutter.

Uncomfortable with her distress, Cooper broke in. "I *don't* know Molly too well, but you know her. Aren't you pretty close, even beyond being relatives? I get that sense. What's up?"

After a pause and another deep breath, the stuttering ended. "The thing is, Cooper, when the kids got sick and I had to talk you into staying overnight at Molly's, I panicked when she first called. I hadn't figured out how to tell her that I needed your help like that, especially since she was so reticent about, well, about hiring you in the first place. I guess you knew that, but it sounds so awful to say out loud, to your face — well, not that it's to your face, really, since we're on the phone, but you know . . ."

As usual, it took her a while, but Nancy eventually caved in and told him everything. Even though Molly had made it crystal clear to Cooper that he was far from her first choice for a nanny, he winced to hear it from Nancy. He'd rather suspect than know for sure that Molly had filled Nancy in on all of her misgivings.

After years of receiving only praise — or, at least, no criticism — Molly's attacks on his abilities unexpectedly hurt. Logically, he had no real skills and no training as a nanny. The confident litigator in him, still very much a part of him, saw that as irrelevant. He hadn't yet met the obstacle, or opponent, that was more than his match.

Cooper started to see where Nancy was going. "Wait. You never called her? You just let the phone ring? I thought you told me on Monday, when you asked me to do this *favor* for you, that you'd clear it with Molly. Unbelievable. Molly's been worried sick about you and your kids."

"I know, I know. I can't believe it, either. Every time the phone rang in the last couple days, my heart stopped. I just didn't know how to explain it to Molly. After all, we'd talked Monday morning before she left, and it wasn't long after that when I realized Kelly and baby Charlie were both sick. Then, once I started freezing up whenever Molly called, it just got worse. It doesn't count for much now, but I'm so sorry, Cooper. Really. None of this was your fault. I should've told you sooner."

What a mess. It looked like he wasn't the only one Molly could be tough on. Even her sister-in-law, an incredibly verbose but nice woman, was so intimidated by Molly that she couldn't admit her kids had chicken pox. How could Molly blame her for that?

He shook his head. "Well, it's done now. No real harm, I guess. I told her your kids had chicken pox, but I think she wanted to hear it from you. Molly probably wanted to throttle me a few times in the last couple days, but the telephone made it a little difficult. She was just worried about you. If she was mad, I'm probably still her main target, but I don't know why."

"Oh, don't worry about it. She'll loosen up — at least, I hope she does. Actually, I can't make any promises. Her ex is a loser, and, other than Steve, she hasn't known many men who weren't. Either bad luck or poor judgment on her part, maybe some of both. I don't really know, and we've been best friends since business school."

If Nancy didn't know, how was *he* supposed to figure Molly out? Cooper wondered, not for the first time, if she was worth the time and trouble of doing that.

In his silence, Nancy kept talking. Which wasn't exactly unusual for her. "With any luck, you can hang on long enough to get to know each other. After all, aren't you supposed to be some tough litigator? You'd never let Molly chew you up, right? I know, I've been pretty awful to you myself, but that's not Molly's fault. Really, I just panicked."

"There have been times in the last few days when my law practice has started to look pretty good. Molly blows hot and cold. Sometimes she's okay, like when she's asking about her kids or you, but other times . . . I've almost asked her if she drinks battery acid for breakfast."

Okay, it wasn't nearly as up and down with Molly as he portrayed. The more they talked, the more she mellowed. They'd gotten off to a bad start on Sunday, but more than a little of that might have been due to her panic over her trip and her surprise at having a man apply to be her nanny. Sure, Molly could be a little uptight even by a lawyer's standards, but he'd had his moments during his years of practicing law. He just wasn't having them now, while he was on "summer break."

"All I can say is that her bark is worse than her bite. Molly's a great friend. I think you'll like her once you get to know her. She isn't as easy to know as someone like . . . like that neighbor of hers, Brooke what's-her-name. But I suspect you're bright enough to figure that out. And Alec and Emma are the greatest, aren't they? Emma can talk your ear off, but they're wonderful. Hang in there. You're probably doing fine so far, and it can only get better."

Suppressing a chuckle, Cooper tried to imagine Emma talking Nancy's ear off. That would be the eighth wonder of the world.

More seriously, he drew a mental comparison between Molly and Brooke. No, Molly wasn't even remotely like Brooke. It didn't take a rocket scientist to figure that one out. He'd like to catch an eyeful — or a handful — of Molly in one of Brooke's bikinis, though.

Time to let Nancy get back to her kids. "I can't say how great I'm doing, but I'm having fun. They're good kids. Thank God for naps, though. Without them I don't think I'd survive. But I've taken too much of your time, Nancy, especially with your kids sick. Tell you what: I'll explain it to Molly. Somehow. You probably won't escape your own inquisition from her, but I'll give it my best shot."

"Thanks, Cooper. Good timing — I think I hear Kelly calling. Good luck with the kids and Molly. I hope you survive a lot more than the day. Wait and see. Take care, now. Talk to you later."

Hanging up, Cooper was glad Molly was supposed to be tied up most of the day today. He knew how Nancy felt, but coming up with a decent explanation for Molly was another thing. So far, all of his experience thinking on his feet in a courtroom didn't help him a bit with Molly. Stymied, he leaned back on the couch, letting sleep overtake him. Bliss.

So far, so good. Nancy had been right, at least this time, about Molly. Calling to check on the kids last night, Molly had sounded surprised and, Cooper suspected, a little hurt when he matter-of-factly explained that Nancy had felt bad about letting her down and couldn't think of a good way to tell her.

Molly must not realize how tightly wound she'd been when she left for New York on Monday morning. It wasn't much of a stretch to imagine her wrath spilling onto the closest object. He'd been irritated with Nancy for not facing up to Molly, but surprised? No.

Molly hadn't been angry, though. Not that he could tell. Maybe, with yet another day like the ones before, she was too tired to send any arrows in his direction. She'd taken it all in stride, her only questions focusing on how Nancy, Steve, and their kids were doing. Normal stuff.

Apparently satisfying herself that all was as well as could be expected, Molly had taken time to speak with both Emma and Alec, then had asked to speak again with Cooper. They'd ended the conversation on a high note, with Molly actually laughing over Cooper's description of Alec's latest antics in the tree house and Emma's attempts to save the doomed baby birds. Cooper stayed on the alert the whole time they spoke, out of habit and a sense of self-protection, but he hadn't needed to shield himself last night. Signing off, they'd exchanged pleasant good-nights.

The morning dawned bright, clear, and

early. Emma's high-pitched titter was Cooper's only warning, mere seconds before Alec landed on his stomach. Any lower and . . . well, not worth thinking about.

After three days of sudden awakenings with these two, Cooper debated the pros and cons of setting his alarm for five a.m. and getting a head start on the game. It might let him plot some semblance of a strategy against Alec and Emma. He sure hadn't had much of a strategy so far, unless constant capitulation was a strategy. On the other hand, it took every ounce of his energy to keep up with the twins, who confounded him whether they were acting in concert or at cross purposes to each other. The need for sleep won out.

Alec's belly flop onto Cooper landed just after five-thirty. So much for sleep. At least Molly would be here in a few hours. Maybe then he could take a break from the action. At a minimum, he'd have reinforcements, and it would be more of a fair fight with two against two.

Heaven help him if it turned out to be one against three. Ouch. He didn't want to contemplate that.

After Emma reminded him of his promise to take them to the park this morning, Cooper helped the kids through another messy breakfast, then out of their pajamas and into shorts and shirts for the day. All of that came after a short delay while Cooper explained to Emma why a ballerina tutu wasn't appropriate attire for the slides and swings at the playground.

Okay, so the delay hadn't been all that short, ending only after yet another bribe to get her to switch to shorts and a T-shirt. She probably didn't even want to wear the tutu in the first place but knew an opportunity for a bribe when she saw one.

Cooper pulled Molly's SUV into the garage a little after ten-thirty. Stepping into the house, he noticed for the first time the orange juice trickling down the side of the counter, the scrambled eggs attached like glue to the wall, and the toast crumbs sprinkled like a fine mist over the entire kitchen floor, table, and chairs. The kitchen sink was piled high with unwashed dishes, spilling over onto the counters. Even by his low standards, the place was a pigsty.

Walking around the first floor, a chagrined Cooper saw what he hadn't noticed in the last three days. The living room, the kids' bedrooms, even Molly's office looked more like the kitchen than not. Less spilled food, maybe, a disaster nonetheless. He hoped the stains he saw could be removed, that all the broken and torn objects weren't beyond repair. He had no idea.

What had happened? Shaking himself, he started toward the kitchen to clean up that hellhole just as Molly walked through the door leading in from the garage. From the look on her face, Cooper wasn't the only one in a state of dazed horror. But he was the one responsible for hers.

"Good God. What on earth did you do to my house?"

CHAPTER SIX

Molly's eyes swept every room, missing nothing, each pass deepening the thunder-cloud that stormed through her in the heartbeat after she walked through the door. Cooper couldn't even look at her. Face her. Make up a lame excuse. He cast his eyes to the floor and dropped into an armchair.

What a nightmare. Relieved that the kids looked unharmed — although sporting mismatched clothes and food in their hair — Molly worked to calm herself so she didn't wind up getting booked for assault.

She tried to remember a more visible disaster with earlier nannies, hoping it would relieve the unbearable churning in her stomach. She couldn't think of a single one. Sure, she'd had plenty of serious problems with her prior nannies, but they paled against the disaster that faced her. Whether the bad memories were fading, or whether she'd forcibly blocked them in her subconscious, she had no idea. She was clear-headed enough to recognize that she wasn't clear-headed at all right now, but . . . for God's sake, she didn't need this. Not after the week she'd had.

And yet . . .

And yet, in the moments before she'd opened the door, Molly had heard the laughter of her children pierce the air, shattering the cloud she'd been under since Monday. Invisible to Alec and Emma, out of sight in the driveway, she knew they'd been genuine in their unfettered happiness.

Molly was all too aware that, more often than not, they experienced that sense of joy only around her, and Steve and Nancy and their kids. Not as often as she'd hope with Drew. Not with many of the nannies she'd had the bad luck to hire, who were either too strict or too absorbed in their own issues, their own lives.

Too much to process. To catch the earlier flight home, she'd had to schedule a crack-of-dawn breakfast meeting today and grab a couple fifteen-minute conversations on the run with business contacts she couldn't afford to miss. On top of a working evening that had ended after midnight, the exhaustion that had seeped into her soul all week still clung. Molly didn't have enough left in her to sort this out. Not now, not today.

Just when she'd started to let down her guard around Cooper. Men. No wonder she couldn't trust any of them. Faced with responsibilities, they acted like a bunch of overgrown children.

Avoiding Cooper, Molly gazed down at the towheaded bookends now attached to her legs. She'd give anything — anything! — to drop headfirst into bed, but they sought their long-promised kisses and hugs and wouldn't be denied. Stooping down to fold them both in her arms, she felt an unexpected benefit as some of the weight of the last few days slipped off her shoulders.

Out of the corner of her eye, Molly noticed Cooper, who looked almost as stunned as she was but not the least bit embarrassed. He even seemed pleased, or at least relieved, to see her. She'd exclaimed only a few words when she walked in, before being stunned into silence. The guy was smart, though; it hadn't taken many words to get his attention. But why had she been forced to experience this disaster before he saw the issue? What *was* it about men?

"Molly, I . . ."

"Look. If you're about to launch into a wild explanation for why the house looks like this and why it's not your fault, I have to tell you, I've heard them all before. From a couple of four-year-olds, from my ex. I don't want to hear it from you. I'm so tired I could die . . . or drop right here on the floor and sleep for twenty hours."

Pausing for effect, Molly gestured at the floor. "No, forget that. I don't think there's a single spot on the floor not covered with food, mud, or whatever that . . . that gooey red stuff is. Gross. Don't tell me. I don't want to know."

Cooper couldn't identify the gross red stuff on the floor, either. From the terrified look on Alec's face, Cooper had a fair idea of its source. But that wasn't the point. Looking back over the last three or four days, he recalled all the times he'd nonchalantly ignored the List, as he'd come to refer to it. His energy more depleted by the frenzied antics of the twins than he'd expected, Cooper had consciously indulged in the games and the outdoor activities. The fun stuff, the stereotypical "guy" stuff. He'd left everything else for another day. For Molly.

Wincing at the awful mess, Cooper realized what he'd done. And what he hadn't. Of course, Molly probably saw this as further justification to cling to her narrow-minded views about men. Pigs. Overgrown children. Yeah, he'd acted like one, but he wasn't one. He also wasn't used to failing. Like too many lawyers he knew, he also wasn't so hot at apologies. Not that Molly was in any mood to accept one.

He'd show her. If she gave him the chance. If she didn't boot his butt out the door in the next two seconds. The bleak look etched on her face, combined with the tired sighs coming out of her right now, made anything a possibility. Not wanting to give her time to think about it, he took action.

"Alec. Emma. You know, guys, your mom is awfully tired. She needs a nap." Seeing the astonished looks on their faces, he smiled. "Yep, believe it or not, grown-ups *like* to take naps. So, why don't we let her go take a nap, and the three of us can do something fun, like cleaning up the kitchen, and the living room, and the hall, and your bedrooms. Yeah! Wouldn't that be great? Boy, that would be *so* much fun, I can't wait. Too bad your mom can't do it, too, but we're going to make her take a nap. Yuck. We get to clean, and she has to nap. But maybe she can have some fun later, though, huh?"

In the space of a few short days, Cooper had discovered an amazing truth about dealing with preschoolers, or at least these particular ones. If his tone of voice, facial expression, and demeanor indicated he was excited about something, they'd do it. No matter how awful. No questions asked. It was tempting to see how far they'd go on that, but he didn't want to press his luck. It worked.

Like right now. Squealing with glee over the fun cleaning they got to do, they forgot about Molly and disengaged themselves from her legs. He might salvage the situation yet.

Molly's reaction to Cooper's overture was less clear. Stunned by the turn of events, her eyes again roamed the room, eventually landing on him. All of him, head to toe.

Cooper felt stripped bare, uneasy, without a clue what direction her thoughts were taking. Normally — even in court — he loved being the focus of a woman's scrutiny, especially when the woman in question physically appealed to him as Molly did. Even after a long week and a tiring trek home, she looked almost as fresh, as crisp, as . . . gorgeous as when she'd left Monday morning. The hair still bounced, the emerald eyes — now darkened with anger or fatigue, or both — still lit up the room.

The short, tight black skirt, chunky black heels, sheer stockings, and sleeveless yellow blouse she wore turned his knees into pudding but aroused other parts of him. The combination gave her the carefree, youthful look of a high-school kid but provoked him to notice her the way he would a sensual, spirited, confident woman who knew what she wanted and how to get it.

From the way her eyes perused him, Cooper would almost think she wanted him. Yeah, she wanted him, all right. Out of the house, probably. Now. She was so tired, she wasn't actually looking at him — not in any physical way — or at anything else, except maybe at the mess he and the kids had made.

He couldn't figure her out in a million years. It didn't matter, anyway. If he could get her to take a nap and forget the household problems he'd totally ignored the last few days, it might buy him enough time to remedy matters. It would also refresh her. Seized by a desire to wipe that wan, broken look off her face, Cooper straightened and walked over to Molly, whose eyes grew larger with every step that brought him closer. Forcibly turning her shoulders in the direction of the stairs to her second-floor master suite, he eschewed the temptation to tap her on her cute little butt, settling instead for a mockingly stern, "You! Upstairs! Now, march!"

Good plan until his wayward hands refused to release her shoulders. For a moment, he held her, letting her flowery scent tease his nostrils. Letting the cool softness of her skin beneath his palms warm him, fanning a spark into a gentle flame. He held her a moment longer. Not long enough.

He'd probably gone too far. Head turned, her glare dissolved and the mumbled protests died on her lips, but her body tensed. And the moment ended. The twins, oblivious and giggling over the spectacle of someone ordering their mother to do *anything,* pushed him aside and fell into line behind her, marching to the beat of . . . well, some drummer somewhere.

She sighed and obeyed. Turning around to shoo Alec and Emma back in Cooper's direction, she smartly saluted the trio and whirled in place, stomping an exaggerated march up the steps. Three jaws dropped as she did.

At the top of the stairs, Molly turned left into her bedroom, shut the door, and collapsed against it. He'd caught her staring. She hadn't intended to, didn't know why she had. Hadn't realized she was doing it until she glimpsed, belatedly, the telltale flush of crimson brightening his cheeks moments before he'd abruptly sent her upstairs. Then he'd held her — okay, held her shoulders — for a few brief seconds. Not knowing what it meant, she'd been only too happy to escape. Another minute downstairs and she might have given in to a sudden and inexplicable urge to run her hands through his hair, to tame the untameable.

Running both hands through her own hair instead, she gazed at the ceiling, deep in thought. What was she doing? She was his employer, for God's sake. He was her employee. And not even much of one, from the looks of things downstairs.

And he was a man. Whew. No doubt about that. Brushing aside the unexpected thrill that shot through her, she focused on all the negatives. Countless negatives. Drew, Jed, even her father. Not Steve, but . . . geez, almost every other guy had always disappointed her. All her life. Cooper had already disappointed her, too. A man's good looks went only so far. They didn't justify buying the rest of the package.

It was time to sleep. There would be time enough later to figure out Cooper. Maybe even figure out her confusing reaction to him. Right now, her brain wasn't up to the challenge.

■ ■ ■ ■

So much for a free afternoon. Cooper glanced around the kitchen, surveying the gleaming counters and stove, the now-spotless refrigerator, the table free of debris. The floor, no longer attractive to multitudes of ants, roaches, and larger critters. The kitchen — the most disgusting of the messes that had awaited his broom, mop, and scouring pads several hours ago — had been put off until last. Done.

The twins had long since tired of the "game" of cleaning the house. After running, climbing, and shrieking themselves into a state of collapse, they toddled off to their respective beds to join Molly in dreamland. Cooper appreciated the respite, finding to no surprise he could tackle the housework faster and with better results without four additional little hands. Sticky, gooey little hands.

Twenty after five. Cooper wondered if a typhoon would have the strength to waken the sleeping Perrell household. Doubtful, from the sound of things.

As that thought faded, and Cooper again picked up the mystery novel that remained fixed on page five, the faint swish of a door opening down the hall registered in his brain. Emma. The little imp always seemed to be on a stealth reconnaissance mission when she emerged from her room, first thing in the morning and after her naps. As she tiptoed down the hall, he stole a quick glance out of the corner of his eye before settling back to page five. He wasn't going to be moving beyond page five anytime soon.

"*Yaaaaaa!* Gotcha! I gotcha, Cooper, didn't I? Didn't I? You never saw me! I'm pretty quiet, aren't I? Aren't I, Cooper?" Practically shouting by the end of the stream of questions, she proved herself more wrong with each additional word, but Cooper didn't have the heart to send her lopsided grin plummeting downward.

"Of course, sweetie. I had no idea you were there. You surprised me. Big time. I bet you're about ready to join the Navy SEALs, you're getting so good."

"A seal? Does the Navy have seals? Why, Cooper? Do they have seals on their big ships? I don't think Mommy would want me to go away and live on a big ship. I swim real good, but I'm not supposed to cross the street without Mommy or you or another grown-up. Aren't ships across the street? I'd have to go real far away. Maybe ten blocks? I don't know. I don't think I want to be a seal. Mommy would be really, really sad if I went away. Unless I came back for lunch."

Struggling to stifle a grin, Cooper debated the pros and cons of explaining Navy SEALs, eventually opting in favor of reducing the inevitable inquisition by skipping the discussion. Someday, though, he'd love to see little Emma in a courtroom. She'd knock 'em dead with her convoluted logic.

For now, Cooper settled for giving her a mock look of concern and ruffling her hair. "Very thoughtful of you, kid. I'll bet your mom would be awfully glad if she knew you'd give up being a SEAL just to stay here with her."

"I *am* awfully glad to hear that. After all, I just got home — I'd hate to have you leave now, too, Pooh-bear."

Looking up sharply, Cooper belatedly realized that the silence of Molly's own footsteps as she'd made her way down the stairs rivaled Emma's. He hadn't heard her approach and didn't know how long she'd been standing there, listening to their silly conversation.

Hair tousled and cheeks flushed from the long nap, Molly was none the worse for wear. Her eyes again sparkled, he noted, preferring the way they gleamed with affection as she stroked Emma's hair over the way they'd sometimes, in his short acquaintance with Molly, glowered at him in fits of annoyance.

She'd also changed into shorts and a sleeveless top, leaving her legs and feet bare. Fresh. Dressed like this, she really did look like a teenager. The sophisticated haircut and the diamond studs she'd forgotten in her ears gave her away, leaving her in the adult world, but Cooper liked the sleek, lithe look of her toned arms and mile-long legs. She must manage to fit regular workouts into her packed schedule. No one could look so effortlessly good without a little effort.

Turning her gaze on him, Molly barely missed the blatant assessment he'd given her. Thankfully. She'd probably eat him alive for a transgression like that, then spit him out.

"Wow. The house looks great again. Thank you. And thanks for occupying the kids while I slept. I feel ten years younger, as though the last several days never happened." Molly slanted him an appreciative smile. A first. Cooper waited, however, for the "but." It came.

"But . . . I don't understand what happened here. Was there something you didn't understand about my instructions? I thought I made everything pretty clear. Or, if something wasn't clear, you could've asked." A perplexed little line creased the center of Molly's brow as she asked the question. Cooper preferred it over the crossed-arms, toe-tapping thundercloud he'd expected.

"I'm sorry. I've had five hours to try to come up with something more eloquent, more defensible, and for once in my life, I'm speechless. I didn't know what I was getting myself in for, and the kids ran me ragged."

Molly just lifted her eyebrows. And didn't say a word.

Standing up, he stuffed his hands in his pockets. "Yeah, I know, I've got thirty years on them, and I still let them run me around. There's no excuse. I kept telling myself that they were having fun, I was having fun — what's the big deal, you know? It wasn't until a few seconds before you walked in the door today that I realized I screwed up. Everything has consequences. As a lawyer, of course, I always knew it. Somehow, I thought those rules didn't apply if I quit being a lawyer."

Seeing the odd look crossing Molly's face,

a retort likely on the tip of her tongue, Cooper bowed his head in defeat. "Yeah, I figured you wouldn't understand. Can't blame you. I don't know the first thing about being a nanny. I'm sorry. I'll grab my stuff and leave now, if you'd like. Or . . . I guess you might need me to stay for a few more days while you find someone else. Well, whatever you want. I don't have anything else lined up."

"Do you always question yourself like this, then answer before a person can get a word in? Is that some lawyer thing? From what I can see, you get to play judge, prosecutor, and defendant all at the same time. Doesn't anyone else get to play?" A smile briefly lit up Molly's features, then faded again while she deliberated over what to do.

While he awaited the verdict, not answering her rhetorical question, he forgot to care about the job situation and wanted another glimpse of that sunburst of a grin. His ego didn't much like the thought of being summarily fired, but he should've thought of that a little sooner.

Forgetting for a moment that Cooper stood there, waiting for her decision, Molly stared heavenward, contemplating her options. She didn't have many. That last ad she'd placed in the newspaper, seeking a nanny, had yielded a plethora of responses. She'd already interviewed all of the plausible ones. Cooper had been her last hope.

Was there any way to make this work? She had no idea. The guy was obviously a great *pal* to Emma and Alec. He had a genuine rapport with little kids. A lot of nannies she'd seen, and too often hired, were skilled but didn't enjoy a real give-and-take with children, especially preschoolers. They made better drill sergeants, cooks, and chauffeurs. Not that an adult was supposed to be their *friend.* Heavens, no. They needed someone to look up to, to listen to and respect, not another playmate. Was Cooper capable of that?

He'd also screwed up — royally. Molly had seldom seen a disaster on the scale of the one Cooper and the kids made while she'd been gone. Imagine being gone longer than a few days! Involuntarily, she shuddered. *Don't go there, Moll.* But he'd realized — belatedly — what he'd done, or not done, as the case may be. He'd admitted it, he'd apologized. A couple times, even. His remorse seemed real. That alone won Cooper huge brownie points.

Guys never said they were sorry. Okay, her brother did once in a while, but Steve had spent so much of their childhood pulling her pigtails and making fun of her braces, he owed her. Drew didn't have the word "sorry" in his vocabulary. Dad didn't, either — Mom was a saint to stay with him all these years. He was a virtual stranger, never having come to her piano recitals, her tennis matches, or anything else that had ever mattered. In high school, she'd joked to her friends that he probably wouldn't find time to make it to her funeral.

So Cooper wasn't as bad as Drew or Dad. It wasn't much of a standard to set for a nanny, though: surpassing the achievements of men who'd never, ever, been there for her. It wouldn't take much.

Molly couldn't avoid the immediate decision any longer. Bottom line, Cooper seemed to like Alec and Emma, and the kids liked him. She might just have to "manage" him a bit better. Give him more instructions, more rigid parameters. Right. Like that had worked the first time.

She could try, anyway. She'd have to give this more thought. For now, though, Cooper was a known quantity, and Molly needed him until she found something better.

"Cooper, I . . ."

"Mommy! You're not going to make Cooper go away, are you? No, no, no, no, no!

We like him! He's fun, and he helped me catch a toad — didn't you, Cooper?" Alec, brushing the sleep out of his eyes, charged the last few steps separating him from Cooper and threw his entire weight against Cooper. Luckily, it wasn't a lot of weight. As it was, the momentum nearly took Cooper down.

"Yesssss, Mommy. Cooper's really neat. He lets me go swimming lots and lots, and we even rode hors — um, the merry-go-round. Yes! Horses on the merry-go-round. At Nickelodeon Universe." Emma's eyes widened to saucers as she spoke, but Molly chose to let it go.

"Shhhh. Hush, you two. Let Mommy talk to Cooper, okay?" She was on the verge of changing her mind, fearing from Emma's guilty face that Cooper really *had* taken the kids horseback riding, but even he wouldn't do something that reckless. She probably just imagined what Emma had been about to say.

The cacophony of the kids' clamoring quieted. Alec still clung to Cooper's legs, Emma to hers, but she could hear herself think.

"I guess it's unanimous. I'd be lying if I said I shared the enthusiasm of my two offspring, but, well, nothing seems to be damaged beyond repair, the kids like you, and I guess you know I need the help."

Cooper sputtered, taking a step backward with Alec still attached. "You want me to stay? After everything? Are you sure? I mean, if you're all right with — sure. I'd be happy to help out."

Regaining his usual aplomb only at the end, Cooper tried valiantly to save face. *Too little, too late,* she thought.

"Let's talk more about things in the morning, if it's okay with you. I'm still a bit beat, and I ought to do something about dinner."

"Sounds fine. I'll be taking off, then."

"Sure. I forgot — I'm not the only one who's had a long week. We'll figure out all your overtime pay, of course, but I wanted to thank you again for staying with Alec and Emma when Nancy and Steve's kids got sick. I really appreciate it." Awareness shot through her of the sacrifices Cooper had made to help her through the week, and Molly wished she could take back some of the things she'd said when she'd been so stressed and so far away from the kids.

It couldn't have been easy for Cooper. New job, no training for it, and . . . *wham.* On duty twenty-four hours a day with two four-year-olds, who couldn't do much of anything for themselves. It was tough on

Molly when she had to do it, and she was their mother, after all. Cooper had probably never done anything even remotely like it. Hours in the courtroom were nothing compared to the same number of hours spent saving Alec, or even Emma, from the mortal danger Alec constantly inflicted on both of them.

She'd been ungrateful and hypercritical to the max. Harsh but true. It wasn't like her — although he probably figured it was — and she'd have to make it up to Cooper. At the same time, though, she had to make sure he put a little more discipline into his time with the kids. She'd be walking a tight-rope.

"No prob." Cooper nodded and started toward the front door, after first disentangling Alec from his legs, then turning abruptly and going down the hall, returning a few minutes later with a large gym bag slung over his shoulder. "So, seven-thirty tomorrow morning?"

"Seven-thirty? Oh. Hmmm. No, we could both — all — use a little sleep after the last few days. Why don't you make it nine? It's Friday, and I can take it easy at work tomorrow." The mention of sleep brought unbidden reminders of her train of thought about Cooper before she'd headed upstairs for her nap. He didn't seem to notice. Good.

"That sounds great. Yeah, I could use it." Turning back to the twins, who tripped over their feet to scoot to him, he bent down and looked from one to the other. "See you tomorrow, munchkins. And don't wake your mom up early. Be good, guys."

Straightening, he made another move toward the door. Emma blew him a two-handed kiss and Alec started to, then thought better of it and turned it into a hasty salute. "Bye, bye, Cooper!" they called out in unison.

"Goodnight, Molly," Cooper said, turning back one last time to offer her a wave.

"See you tomorrow. And thanks again." Watching as he ambled toward the front door, she enjoyed the luxury of admiring the view from behind without him catching her in the act. He was a stunner, with his broad shoulders tapering downward into an athletic, narrow waist and hips. Okay, he also had a cute butt. Couldn't forget that, as Nancy would say. Thank God Nancy was so blissed out by that brother of hers. Maybe she wouldn't notice Cooper and wouldn't start pushing Molly in his direction.

Ha. Too much to hope.

Speaking of hope, Molly hoped she wasn't

pushing herself in Cooper's direction. Hoped she hadn't made the decision not to get rid of him based on anything other than her dire need for a nanny. She'd always had a clear head for business, and hiring a nanny was just business. With Cooper, why did she have to keep reminding herself of that?

No wonder Cooper warned them not to wake me too early. Wincing as Alec forcibly pried open one of her eyelids and Emma grasped her toes and pulled — hard — Molly mentally prepared herself to face the new day. Five a.m. Ugh.

Sleep had come, begrudgingly, only after hours spent pondering the fates and her awful luck with nannies. Not many women would consider Cooper awful luck. Quite the opposite.

Twenty-nine years old, she'd succeeded at work beyond her wildest expectations, beginning only a few short months after she'd gotten her MBA. She'd leapfrogged to the top, passing many highly qualified people who had both age and experience on her. A few resented her for it — but, luckily, not too many of those.

But men? Nothing had ever gone right on that front. A couple of long-term steadies in college — nice, smart, but lacking something. That sense of romance, of *passion,* she'd heard about from friends and seen on the big screen. Something that went beyond the physical — a soul-deep joining. She'd never gotten much further than some kissing and awkward groping and late-night debates over political candidates, none of whom mattered at all to her now and, if she'd been honest, hadn't much at the time.

Then came Drew. So sophisticated, so handsome, so smug. So irritating. So manipulative. So caught up in himself, he'd found caring, simple affection, and faithfulness impossible. He'd seemed so worldly and polished compared to the men — boys, really — she'd dated in college and grad school. Drew had appeared on the scene, almost by magic, a month before her final paper had been due, before she'd gotten her MBA. Armed with an MBA and sundry other degrees of his own, a gleaming Jaguar, and an even brighter future in his dad's investment banking firm, Drew seemed to possess everything she'd ever wanted.

Her friends saw through him in a couple weeks. For Molly, it took a bit longer. Unfortunately, the lightbulb flashed on in her brain when she was already pregnant with Emma and Alec. Her two precious angels meant everything in the world to her, and had from the moment she'd known they were inside her. They'd thrown a wrench in any plans she might otherwise have pursued to dump Drew, but it wasn't their fault. It was hers for being so blind. She wouldn't let a man blind her again.

As she'd tossed and turned last night, Molly thought about Cooper, even wished he'd been tossing and turning right along with her. Yes, she definitely smiled as she entertained that wicked thought, but she stopped short of pursuing it much further than kissing. Okay, maybe a little hugging, touching, tasting, too. Possibly a little more than that. Fighting her reawakened imagination, she cursed the thoughts that drenched her with sweat and left her with nothing else to show for it. Next thing she knew, she'd be asking Brooke for pointers.

A little after two a.m., Molly had fought her stray musings into submission, using the same techniques she sometimes used on her business colleagues. Still, it left her with no answers, too many forbidden and unsatisfied longings, and a whopping three hours of sleep. Sheesh. What she wouldn't give for kids who stayed in bed until seven or eight. Or six. She'd settle for six.

Cooper rang the doorbell promptly at nine, looking freshly showered, shaved, and scrumptious. So much for Molly's ability to control her mental gymnastics.

"Hi. How's everyone this morning?" Cooper greeted her answered hello with a grin.

Molly smiled back. "Other than it being a little *early* out this morning when a couple kids I know attacked me, we're all great. How are you doing?"

"Never better. Even without the little munchkins, I woke up a little earlier than I'd like, but I think they trained me to their way of thinking in just a few short days. Hopefully, that's a skill I can unlearn. I'm going to practice tomorrow." Cooper grinned again, clearly refreshed.

Molly, dressed for work and ready to slip past him out the door, shrugged an apology. "Listen, I know I said we'd talk more this morning, but I forgot about a meeting that had been scheduled. Sorry about that. Maybe I can scoot out of work early today. Would that work for you?"

"Yeah, sure. Whatever. We'll be fine. See you later." Despite the growing thaw in their relationship, he looked relieved to postpone any conversation with her. His dreams last night must have been different from hers.

"Thanks. Bye, Cooper. Bye-bye, Alec. Bye-bye, Emma. Love you!" With that, she disappeared through the door into the garage, slid into her BMW, and eased down the driveway. Back to work.

Just past two, Cooper plopped into a lawn chair by the pool, weary after hours of endless games in which Alec and Emma were the pursuers and he was the pursued. Their arsenal of weapons included pillows, garden hoses, and tomatoes plucked directly off Molly's vines. Dripping wet and a little sticky, he considered joining the twins in the pool, where they splashed happily in the shallow end.

Cooper wore the Bermuda shorts and T-shirt he'd changed into after the ketchup episode during lunch. Shortsighted, he rued having brought only one extra set of clothes today. On his fifth day with these hoodlums, he should've known better.

"Cooper! Is that you?" Brooke frantically waved at him over the slatted wooden fence dividing the two yards.

"Right here." *Who else would it be?* he added to himself, sarcastically, as he slowly turned toward her and stood. Brooke still waved, less frantically now that she had his attention. Poured into a halter top and short shorts, and tottering on high-heeled straps that he supposed passed for sandals, he couldn't imagine what she wanted. Or why it involved him.

"Thank goodness. I didn't know *what* to do. My, ah, my brother left the hose hanging from the tree limb. It's stuck, and I can't seem to reach it. Could you help out?"

"Sorry, but not right now. I need to watch the kids. They're in the pool, you know." Looking over at them, in two feet of water, Cooper knew they weren't in any danger, especially with water wings on their arms. Still, he couldn't take his eyes off them for more than a couple seconds, max, and he couldn't figure out why someone — her brother? — would put a hose in a tree, let alone leave it there. Sounded odd, even for Brooke. Maybe her whole family was desperate for attention.

"Oh, Cooper, it'll just take a moment. I'll watch the kids like a hawk while you get the hose. Promise. They're fine. They won't even notice you're gone!"

That was probably true, but he glanced at them again, keeping one eye on them as he walked over to the now-open wooden gate in the fence and peered up at the hose in the tree, which stood just on the other side of the fence. Brooke left her yard and came right up to him, craning her neck to stare at the hose, too.

"Don't you have a ladder? Or a pole? A rake, even?" How was he going to reach the hose, especially with her standing right next to him? Maybe he could yank it down from where he stood. "And remember, you were going to watch the kids."

She didn't move except to shrug helplessly at his questions. Unbelievable.

After another quick glance at the kids, and with Brooke hovering way too close, he reached up toward the branch with one hand, grabbing the hose with the other.

Before he could retrieve the hose, he felt her grab him around the waist. Aim a kiss at his mouth, which he dodged by jerking his head sideways. Wrap the free end of the hose around them both, like a lasso.

What the hell?

In the next instant, an ominous shadow fell over the ground where he stood, wrapped up in a hose with Brooke, and a decided chill invaded the otherwise sunny, eighty-degree day. Molly.

"Am I interrupting anything important?"

CHAPTER SEVEN

At Molly's abrupt question, Cooper let go of the branch and tried to disentangle himself from the hose and Brooke. Turning to face Molly, he twisted himself up even more in the hose and, struggling to free himself, tripped and fell face-first at Molly's feet. They tapped the ground beside his face.

Looking up from his prone position, Cooper didn't mind the impromptu peep show but decided, for the sake of longevity — of his current job and his life span — he'd better assume a vertical position in a hurry. As he drew himself up to his full height, brushing the grass off his knees along the way, Cooper frantically tried to formulate a response.

From his perspective, it was completely innocent. From Brooke's perspective, he now knew, a different story altogether. A sidelong glance confirmed, too late, that this must've been a setup. Her expression quickly went from helpless to leering, a smug smile of satisfaction planted on her face.

How could he be such a chump? All those straight A's back in school, and he was a freaking idiot. How could anyone get a hose stuck in their tree? Why would he fall for such a stupid line? God, what a sucker he'd been. "Folly." Oh, God. Had he really just said that? He cleared his throat, a temporary substitute for yanking out his tongue. "I mean, *Molly,* it's not what you think." *Great. Isn't that what the guilty ones always say?* Cooper dragged in a deep breath. "Look. I just came over two seconds ago, when Brooke said the hose was caught in her tree. Isn't that right, Brooke?"

Brooke remained silent, grinning like a Cheshire cat.

"I'm so glad we have that cleared up. And who, exactly, was watching my kids *in the pool* while Brooke's poor hose was . . . caught?" Molly glared from one to the other. Her disbelief and jealousy rang through loud and clear. Dislike and distrust of men — of him — oozed from her every pore.

It figured. Disgusted with Brooke, sick to death of Molly's accusations and groundless suspicions, Cooper turned to walk back to the far end of the pool. As he did, he shot Molly a quick glance over his shoulder. "I never left your yard, Molly, and I kept my eye on the kids. It was under control. The kids are fine."

More than I can say for you, he muttered under his breath.

"What?" Molly called after him.

At the pool, Cooper retrieved a ball that sailed past him, then bent down to pitch it lightly back at Emma, the culprit of the moment. "Nothing, Molly. Nothing at all."

"I said — what was it you said?"

"And I said — nothing. What is it with you, anyway? Can't you ever give it a rest?"

"I heard what you said." She might be bluffing. Better for her to guess, but not know for sure, than for him to repeat it. "What do you mean — 'give it a rest'? Who are you to say that to me?" Molly asked that last question with her arms crossed, head tilted to the side, eyebrows lifted.

"Cooper Meredith, ma'am, at your service. That's who. But don't worry. I won't be at your service for long. I can take a lot of abuse, but being accused of neglecting Alec and Emma, let alone endangering them, is beyond outrageous. If you really believe I'm capable of that, I'm out of here."

Both of them boiling over in rage, they

stood, glaring at each other in a standoff of wills, ignoring their two little spectators. Before Cooper could react, Alec and Emma each drew back and slammed their chubby hands against the water, creating a wall of spray that nailed their respective targets — Cooper and Molly — and soaked them from the waist down.

"Oh! What — ?" Obviously flustered by the unexpected soaking of her silk skirt, Molly sputtered and forgot for a moment all about Cooper. Leaning over the pool and fixing her gaze on Emma and Alec, she started to scold them when both whipped around to paddle away, inadvertently drenching the top half of her — thoroughly — as their little legs churned against the water.

"Come back here, you two. Now!" Molly visibly struggled to regain control, as well as to fight back a grin at the interruption by the imps.

Cooper felt his anger fade as he got caught up in the duo's watery antics. His head back, he laughed and clapped for them. Sensing the adults' changed attitudes, Emma and Alec paddled back to the side of the pool, increasing as they did so the frantic kicks and splashes. Until —

"Uh, oh, Mommy. You're all wet!" As soon

144

as she exclaimed it, Emma clapped a hand over her mouth, realizing who had created that circumstance.

"I — oh, God. Look at me. I mean —" It was too late for Molly to amend her words. As she dripped onto the patio, Cooper needed no encouragement. The yellow silk skirt and matching blouse, which had earlier fluttered gently in the breeze, now clung to Molly's figure, outlining her softly rounded curves against the backdrop of the bright midafternoon sun.

Cooper's imagination — which became more vivid each time he saw Molly — was happily replaced by the real thing. Molly, bright pink now, stood frozen in panic. Cooper's gaze missed nothing, his innate politeness and chivalry lost in his fascination with the way her blouse molded against her. Her stylish clothes, when soaked, failed almost completely to conceal the curves beneath them.

At Molly's waist, the yellow silk swirled against her skin, teasing the gentle curves of her hips, and her slim but lightly muscled thighs pressed against the thin material as the sunshine glimmered behind her. Cooper softly whistled in appreciation, then looked up in horror — matched by the mortification on Molly's face — as it dawned on him what he just did.

"Mommy, don't you wanna dry off? You can use my towel." Alec, no longer fearing any consequences from the bath he'd given Molly, peered up at her, oblivious to the tension between Molly and Cooper.

"Uh — thanks, sweetie. Yes, that would be great. I think I will." Finally drawing upon her reserves of dignity, Molly calmly plucked a large towel from the nearest chair. As she briskly rubbed it down the front of her outfit, then drew it around her shoulders and clutched it together in front, she turned and spoke to Cooper. Her cool, clipped tone indicated her hope that they both pretend neither of them noticed what just happened.

"We need to talk, Cooper. I'll get out of these wet clothes — uh, I mean, I'll change into dry clothes first. Right after that?"

Still focused on the . . . wet . . . clothes, Cooper's mind drifted, momentarily trying to recall what it was they needed to discuss. "Fine. Yeah, whatever. Take your time."

"You might want to change, too. I'm not the only one who suffered at the twins' hands and feet."

Unaware until then of the wet state of his shorts, Cooper looked down at them and shrugged. "I'm afraid I'm stuck with the drip-dry method. I brought only one change of clothes, and a tangle with the wrong end of a ketchup bottle already nailed me. The sun ought to take care of it pretty fast, though."

"Okay. Be right back."

Molly strode to the sliding-glass door, pulled it open, and walked into the house, waiting until she was safely ensconced in her room to throw herself on the king-size bed and abandon her pretense of dignity. *Oh. My. God.* He must have seen *everything*. She winced at her earlier decision not to wear a slip due to the heat.

On the other hand, he hadn't exactly been disgusted, if his little whistle was any indication. Retracing her thoughts of last night, Molly compared the look of amazement in Cooper's eyes just now with the look she'd imagined in her wakeful dreams. Shivering with a flash of desire, Molly stretched out on the bed, arms languorously pulled above her head, and smiled. Moments later, she bounced off the bed, opened her dresser, and changed into a cropped shirt and trim shorts.

Telling herself the abbreviated outfit was strictly for the hot day, she skipped down the stairs. In the kitchen, where Cooper and the twins were munching on animal crackers and juice, she directed Alec and Emma to move their snacks to the basement play-room, leaving Cooper and her free to talk without needing to filter anything for young ears.

With the twins downstairs, Cooper and Molly remained in the kitchen, facing each other warily like animals waiting for the other to charge. Neither wanted to start the conversation. A new tension buzzed between them, one that Molly didn't completely understand or want to explore.

"So." Molly reminded herself that she was the employer, and this was supposed to be an employment relationship. It was up to her to make this work. "We seem to have a lot of issues. I'm not quite sure how to resolve them."

"Maybe you could enlighten me as to exactly what those *issues* might be. I'm not sure I know." Folding his arms against his chest, Cooper appeared to ready himself for battle.

Surprised by his curt tone, Molly paced the room, flexing her fists as she did. "Let's see. Housekeeping, for one. Proper meals. Probably, if I knew more about what went on this week — which might frighten me to think about — activities, nap times, you name it. Safety? Like, oh, around the pool?

Not to mention Brooke . . .”

Cooper was, at first, annoyed as he listened to the litany of his supposed faults. Some of them had a basis in fact, sure, but they didn't capture the *wonder* of the time he'd experienced with the kids. In just a few days, Cooper felt like he was growing, leaving behind the legal world as he explored what now felt like the *real* world with a couple of lively, fun, lovable little four-year-olds at his side.

Emma and Alec reminded him of too many things he'd left behind: a magical world filled with tufts of grass and ribbons of sky, the tickle of a summer breeze, the playful caress of a stream as it babbled over little hands, the deadly purpose of a spider as it captured a fly.

Yeah, naps and bedtime had happened only when all three of them had been dead on their feet, unable to charge up another hill or climb another tree limb. He wasn't the world's greatest cook, but the kids seemed none the worse for it. And after all, he'd been thrown into the deep end, having to come up with three meals a day while Molly was out of town. As for housekeeping — okay, that was a disaster, but he cleaned it up. Eventually.

But Brooke shouldn't be part of this discussion. Unless *he* was the one complaining.

Furious at Molly's accusation, Cooper's eyes narrowed, his nostrils flared. He'd done nothing wrong and had no reason to apologize. Molly obviously thought otherwise. Why couldn't women ever see things the way men saw them? Now, *that* would be a miracle. Brooke wasn't worth the time it took to think about her. That should be obvious to Molly.

All she saw was Cooper, standing in Molly's own yard, trying to get a stupid hose out of a tree on Brooke's side of the fence. Helping out Molly's neighbor. Until, yeah, Brooke grabbed him, tried to kiss him, and who knows what she was trying to do with the hose. In hindsight, he pictured the gleam in Brooke's eyes, the hurt in Molly's. But with a woman next door who looked and acted like Brooke, how could a woman as gorgeous as Molly feel she had to watch her back?

Who knew? All Cooper knew was that he'd stumbled upon something here — a special bond with Alec and Emma, a glimmer of something with Molly. He wanted to explore it, to finish it. He didn't know where it would lead.

He didn't plan to beg, though.

"I guess we do have some issues, Molly. You've figured out I'm not the world's best housekeeper, that I don't know a soufflé from a saucepan. But you have a couple of great kids, and they have fun with me. Just ask them."

"Oh, right, like I'm going to do that. That's like asking if they like candy. Tastes great, but it's not exactly good for them."

"You'd be surprised what's good for them. I may not know everything there is to know about kids, but they seem to do all right with me. From bits and pieces I heard from them this week, that's not a common occurrence with all of your nannies." Molly visibly flinched as he threw that at her. Too bad.

"What about —"

"What about Brooke? Give me a break." Cooper wanted to avoid an argument over Brooke. Hell. He wanted to avoid Brooke altogether. But he needed Molly to trust him, to take him at his word. As a lawyer, he demanded the trust of his clients and opponents. If Molly couldn't give him that, how could she trust him with her kids?

"Don't give me that. I saw her. She was all over you." Even Molly winced at that. Her attempt to feign disinterest gone now, she didn't even bother claiming to be merely a concerned parent.

Cooper wasn't going to convince her. He wouldn't try. Not now, before Molly had a chance to know him. "Listen, I'm not going to defend myself. Brooke is a piece of work, yeah, but think whatever you want. At the end of the day, this isn't about Brooke. It's about whether you want me to stay on as the kids' nanny. That's it."

No response. Molly's pacing continued, punctuated rhythmically by the ticking of the clock over the sink.

She had no viable alternatives, at least not right now. She had to make herself treat Brooke as merely the nuisance she always was and push aside any thoughts of Cooper that were unrelated to his position as her nanny. The latter was possible. Maybe unrealistic, considering the thoughts she'd entertained in his direction, but possible.

Brooke had been all over Cooper. Cooper *hadn't* been all over Brooke.

Not that she should care, anyway. But he hadn't been.

She couldn't think about it. Right now, Molly had to be the adult. Again. Focused strictly on the well-being of her kids. Cooper had his rough edges as a nanny, but his interest in them was genuine, and they liked him. For the moment, that would have to be enough.

Abruptly stopping her pacing in the middle of the kitchen floor, she finally looked at him. Straight in the eye. Firmly. Despite what she felt inside. "You're right. My kids are all that matter. Your extracurricular activities aren't my concern; my children are. But when you're on the clock, they're your only concern too. If that's too tough for you to handle, I need to know now, before we go any further."

Molly grasped the edge of the counter as she awaited his response.

It came without hesitation. "Of course. I'm here for Alec and Emma. No one else."

No one else. From the look of Cooper's firmly pressed lips, Molly knew that included her. Served her right. He probably had no interest in her anyway — at least, not when she was in dry clothes. She'd sealed his decision with her jealous little tantrum about Brooke.

So be it. She couldn't and wouldn't compete with Brooke, not over a man who would only let her down or break her heart someday. Better for her to remember what he'd said: he was here for the kids.

The ground rules needed clarifying,

though. Compliance with them had to improve dramatically as well. "While we're at it, we need to talk about how you handle the twins — food, schedules, activities, all of that. For me to become more comfortable about this whole situation, it can't be Camp Chaos every time I come home."

Cooper sat at the kitchen table, at least pretending patience, as she reeled through a monologue of things he should or shouldn't do. Although he grabbed a notepad partway through her lecture, jotting notes, she wasn't fooled for an instant. He probably wouldn't follow more than a quarter of it. But, for now, their shaky truce held.

The weekend couldn't come too soon. Molly let Cooper go a little after four. Whether she'd finally run out of directions, or out of steam, he didn't know and didn't care. Friday night brought Cooper to the downtown after-work scene — something, with his unending workload, he hadn't experienced much in the last several years — barhopping with Jake and a few of the other unattached lawyers from the Pemberton firm, moving from Zelo to the Local to Brit's Pub and back again.

Finally, a little after ten, Jake and Cooper were the last ones left. It was their first chance to talk about Cooper's new job.

"So how's it going, big guy? How are the wild-and-crazy suburbs? Race any minivans around the neighborhood?"

"Yeah, right. It's not that bad." Cooper didn't miss Jake rolling his eyes. "And cut it out. I know it's pretty weird, and I don't know what I'll do long term. On the other hand, I haven't thought about a case all week. No briefs, no arguments, no hearings. Nothing. Nada. Zippo. It feels great."

Cooper needed someone from his former life to understand, even if they didn't agree. He suspected that person wouldn't be Jake, even though Jake was his best friend.

Surprisingly, Jake nodded. "Even better, no Garrison. You wouldn't believe what the old guy's doing. I swear, your leaving pushed him over the edge. He's been on the rampage for one thing or another all week. I caught the brunt of it, but a couple of associates threatened to quit today. Neither mentioned anything about becoming a nanny, though . . ."

Jake dulled the edge of that last cut with a wink and a grin. He just didn't dull it enough.

"You know, it's not the worst —"

"Aw, come on, Coop. Just teasing you, man. I admit I don't understand, but we've been through a lot over the years. Don't go stressing on me." Punching Cooper in the arm, Jake leaned back on his barstool, his eyes meandering over the packed room.

Cooper took a long pull on his beer. "Yeah, okay. Why should you understand it when I can't figure it out myself? So what's up with you? I don't miss the firm, but it already seems like months since we've talked."

"Same old. I've been seeing Mariah for a couple months. Off and on, of course — wouldn't want her to start relying on me or anything." This time, Jake's accompanying wink looked more forced. "Apparently, she's found someone she *can* rely on. Broke our date last night, claiming a headache. Clint Halliday must've cured it, though, since I heard the two of them were together at the Dakota last night. Pretty cozy. I called her today, and we broke it off. Guess she was tired of the weekly bar scene with me, never knowing when I'd call."

Despite Jake's rep for partying and frequent changes of female companions, there was more to him than that. Cooper knew it better than anyone, and the look on Jake's face confirmed it. He also knew Jake wouldn't want any sympathy. Maybe he'd settle for a distraction instead.

"If you're in the market for some fresh blood, I may have just the woman for you." Brooke might be a bit much even for Jake, but she was nothing if not a distraction for someone who wanted one.

"I don't know, Coop. Who is it? Your new boss?"

Cooper's heart clenched at the thought of Jake with Molly. Picturing Brooke with Jake, and partly in jest, he hadn't been thinking of Molly at all.

Not for, oh, at least five minutes.

"Uh, no. She's . . . um, you wouldn't — what I mean is, she's not your type. I'm talking about Molly's next-door neighbor. Quite a woman." Struggling to put together a complete sentence, Cooper's face flushed and he couldn't meet Jake's eyes.

"Yeah, right. If she's so hot, why aren't you after her? But what's this with 'Molly'? Last I heard, she was Ms. Perrell, the boss from hell, who practically didn't let you get a foot in the door. Now we're on a first-name basis? What's going on?"

Cooper saw the glimmer in Jake's eye. His own hesitation must've sealed Jake's conclusion. Except for the day he first met Molly, he hadn't been unsure of himself since the first five minutes of oral arguments, first year in law school.

"It's not what you think. She's my employer. Barely that, even. I just survived her tenth threatened termination of me this week, and I could be out on my butt by Monday. She's also not my type." Cooper's collar felt too tight. Reaching up to loosen it, he remembered he was wearing a polo shirt, unbuttoned.

"Not your type. Right. So she's tough. Last I knew, you didn't frighten easily. What gives?" Jake eyed Cooper speculatively.

It was probably Jake's turn to razz him about a woman. God knew, he'd done it to Jake often enough. "Really, Jake, it's nothing. Nothing to report. So give it a rest, okay?"

"Whatever you say, chief."

Jake let it drop, but Cooper knew he wouldn't forget it. In the few words he coughed up, he'd revealed more than he wanted to. Idiot.

Monday morning. Cooper steeled himself for another week. Not with the kids — they were easy — but with Molly. In town all week, she would work harder to keep tabs on him than she'd been able to last week. He was more right than he expected.

"Hi, Cooper. How was your weekend?" She didn't pause for an answer. "Sorry to be in such a rush this morning — although, come to think of it, I guess that's nothing new. I'll be jammed up all morning, but I've got a couple hours free at lunch. I thought we could all go on a picnic. Maybe twelve-thirty or so? Sound okay?" Seeing his faint nod, she called out, "Great. See you," as she strode down the hall and out the door.

Two little faces, smeared with jam, peered up at Cooper. Their owners tugged on his shorts. "Cooper! What do we get to do today?"

Still dazed by Molly's whirlwind exit, Cooper shook his head, clearing it. "What? Oh, yeah, what sounds good to you? Story time at the library, maybe?"

"We like your stories better, Cooper."

Alec nodded his head, echoing agreement with his sister. "Yeah. They're the best."

"Okay. Maybe one. But then let's find a fun place to go. The zoo?"

"Yessss!" they shouted in unison, clapping their hands.

Hours later, worn out from a morning of stories, animals, and frolics in the park, the twins' eyelids were drooping. Cooper figured they were hungry but needed a nap even more. Twelve-fifteen. Belatedly, he realized he should have thrown fewer activities at the kids this morning, to save their energy for the picnic. He wondered why Molly wanted to have a picnic today, when she was probably buried in work, catching up from being out of town last week. That was what he'd always experienced, as a lawyer, coming back from a business trip.

Molly's heels clattered up the sidewalk. He hoped she planned to exchange them for something more practical, or she'd spend half the time at the picnic pulling her heels out of the soft grass.

"Hi, everyone. Ready for a picnic, Emma? Alec?" Molly paused at the door of the kitchen, looking around expectantly, not noticing the drowsy state of its occupants.

"Hi, Mommy. Are we going on a picnic? Will there be horses?" Emma's great love in life never changed.

"No, sweetie. No horses. But I thought it might be nice to go to the park and have a picnic. Doesn't that sound fun?"

Alec shook his head and yawned. "Do we *have* to? I don't wanna go on a picnic."

Ruffling his hair, Molly smiled. "I think it'll be lots of fun. Come on, let's go."

Cooper saw Molly's disappointment in the lack of enthusiasm written plainly on the kids' faces. Wanting to help, without admitting that the morning's activities probably provoked the disinterest, he bent down to their eye level. "Hey, a picnic sounds great. And your mom came all the way home just to take you. If you don't go, she'll be really sad."

Molly cringed at his tactics. Both children perked up slightly, though, and started putting on their shoes.

"Are you going, Cooper, huh, are you?" Alec, Cooper's little shadow, wasn't above pleading to get what he wanted.

"Gee, I don't know, guys. Maybe your mom wants you all to herself." Turning to Molly, he inclined his head. "Would you like that, Molly? I can hang out here."

Frowning, Molly shook her head. "No, I figured we could all go, maybe give us a chance to get to know each other better. Is that okay?"

"Sure. Fine by me." Grabbing Emma by the hand while Molly reached for Alec, he headed for the door into the garage. "Okay, troops. Let's head out."

At the park, the twins' boundless energy returned. Less than an hour passed, however, before Molly conceded that the picnic had been a lousy idea. A colossal mistake. Alec was right. They should've skipped the picnic and stayed home.

Everything had gone wrong. In her rush

to get home from work, Molly had grabbed the custom-made picnic basket the neighborhood grocery had packed for her, for once in her life not stopping to check to see that it was right. The caviar, pâté, and eggplant quiche were probably delicious, but a couple of four-year-olds disagreed. Alec disagreed vehemently. He threw the pâté at Emma, wiped the caviar down the sides of his shorts, and planted his foot smack-dab in the center of the quiche.

Whoever got the juice boxes, cartoon fruit cups, and Wonder Bread sandwiches in the picnic lunch Molly had ordered was probably in for quite a surprise too.

Twenty minutes into the picnic, Emma — with pâté smeared all over her overall shorts — had tripped over a fallen branch and skinned both knees. Not badly, but enough to make her wail so loudly it was a miracle the police hadn't arrested Molly for child abuse.

Later, after Cooper tried to save the day by racing the twins to the ice-cream truck and popping for cones all around, the clouds that threatened all morning let loose with an unexpected torrent of rain. It soaked through their clothing before they could gather the remnants of their picnic and make a mad dash to the SUV.

A soggy trip home followed. Once there, Molly scrambled to pull together some lunch for the still-ravenous Alec and Emma before helping them toddle off to bed for their afternoon nap, drooping so much they forgot to object.

While Molly found dry clothing for the twins to sleep in and changed into some of her own, Cooper cleaned up the aftermath of both lunch and the picnic, the latter dumped on the kitchen floor in his haste to help Molly fix lunch.

Returning to the kitchen to finish her own lunch, Molly stood at the sink, hands propped against the counter. Leaning her head back to relieve the strain in her neck, she sighed and wondered aloud what possessed her to force the picnic on the twins, or even to think of it in the first place.

"Aw, come on. It wasn't so bad." Seeing her look of sheer disbelief, Cooper corrected himself. "Okay, so maybe it was. But who could have predicted it?"

"I should've known better. You're trying to set your own routine with the kids. I shouldn't have interfered with that." Molly bowed her head. "I'm sorry. I thought we could have a nice time. You know, find a way to get past some of our arguing last week. It was a dumb idea."

Walking over to Molly, Cooper gently touched her chin, forcing her to look up at him.

"Molly, nothing you did was dumb at all. It was a great idea, but the fates conspired against you. It's time I admitted I inadvertently helped matters along. The kids and I did so much stuff this morning, I'm surprised they made it as long as they did without falling asleep. I —"

Still downcast, Molly searched his eyes as he made the admission, then waited for him to complete his sentence.

As he spoke, though, Cooper had been staring at Molly — at her cheek? — oddly.

"Molly, there's some — here, let me get that off your face." Touching her cheek, Cooper swiped his finger across it, a quick movement that tingled more than it should've. As Molly stared, fascinated, he held up his finger to show her a tiny dab of cream cheese before sticking his finger in his mouth, sucking on the cream cheese. Staring back, Cooper's gaze fixed on Molly's lips.

She waited, watching him, as he tilted his head downward to meet hers. His lips lightly brushed against hers, then captured them.

Completely.

CHAPTER EIGHT

Soft. Sweet. Cooper's lips, his kiss, surpassed what Molly's midnight musings had predicted. Startled, she forgot to resist.

In fact, Molly forgot everything. That she shouldn't lean, ever so slightly, into Cooper's embrace. Shouldn't sigh when, encouraged by her lack of resistance, Cooper increased the pressure of his kiss, causing her mouth to respond in a way no one had ever tempted it before. Shouldn't whisper a tiny "oh, yes" against his mouth.

Molly forgot every litany of self-restraint she'd ever repeated to herself.

Cooper's hands, which first gently cupped her face before gliding down her throat to grasp her shoulders, now feathered down Molly's sides, his palms teasing her. His thumbs brushed against the wisps of lace not covered by her sleeveless silk blouse.

Ecstasy. Need. Myriad emotions crashed over Molly as her eyes fluttered closed, her head leaned back, exposing her neck to Cooper's lips. A thousand pinpoints of sensation skittered over Molly, making her feel alive in a way she hadn't in so, so long. Opening her eyes, she let them drift over Cooper, taking in his intense concentration as his lips cruised past the hollow at the base of her throat.

As if aware of her gaze, Cooper paused for a moment, an unspoken question flickering in his eyes as he gazed steadily at Molly.

Molly's answer came without thought, without analysis, as she wrapped her arms around his waist, eased herself closer to him, and let her lips do their own exploration.

Cooper didn't wait for any further answer. His hands abandoned all pretense of gentleness as his fingers splayed through her hair, caressed her cheek, boldly held her. Molly felt her body straining against the lace, through the fabric of her shirt, as Cooper's mouth continued its quest.

Flushed, breathless, Molly wanted more. When she felt Cooper's hands on her hips, on her skin, as they played with the bottom hem of her shirt, Molly's desire wrestled with her control. What if . . . what if the children saw them? What was she *doing* with her nanny? Who was this woman who had taken over her body, her mind?

In a matter of moments, Molly's self-doubts took over.

What was she to Cooper, anyway?

Eyes snapping open, Molly glared at Cooper before straightening to her full five foot six, unsuccessful in her futile attempt to look down her nose at the man towering over her.

Cooper's brows furrowed as he took a step back from Molly. Head tilted, he studied her, as if looking into her and through her. Molly couldn't blame him. She wasn't giving him a consistent message, and she was glad he didn't point it out. A typical lawyer might have done that. She knew she deserved it.

What was she supposed to do? She wanted him. She didn't want to, but there it was, impossible to deny. For her children's sake, and maybe for hers, she couldn't let herself lose control like this, lose herself in love — lust — for a man who might turn out to be no different from Drew, from all the rest.

She didn't think Cooper would stay around even long enough to toy with her *properly,* for God's sake. He would go back to his law firm, or some woman from his past — or present, for all she knew — or on to a new one. Like they all did. "Poor little

Molly," or the "ice princess," as she knew Brooke referred to her, wouldn't interest a man like Cooper. She could wow the retail world, maybe even her kids once in a while, but men? No. She was neither the challenge nor the hot commodity they sought.

"What's wrong, Molly?" As always, Cooper's question cut to the chase.

"I don't want — that is, I don't think this is . . . well, appropriate. You know. The children. Work. I employ you. I mean — well, you know." Flustered, Molly waved her hands in circles, trying to explain with them what her tongue couldn't.

Cooper leaned against the kitchen counter, crossing his arms against his chest, one leg over the other, with studied casualness. "No, I'm not sure I do know what you mean. Sure, I'm your employee. I don't think that's what made you stop what was happening between us."

"There's nothing between us. I mean, it might have looked like it, but I —" Seeing Cooper's look of sheer disbelief, Molly plunged on. "Well, I never intended for that to happen. I didn't plan it."

"You didn't *plan* it? What — do you plan everything you do? You kissed me, Molly. You can't just take that back. It *happened*. It's between us."

The lies on Molly's tongue only made her bristle more. "I never asked you to kiss me. Maybe I didn't stop you right away, but I didn't want this. I can't afford to let it happen. None of it. If you want to continue as my kids' nanny, you have to forget this ever happened."

Cooper stared at her, not responding.

The silence ate at Molly. "Well? Does that work for you? If it doesn't, you'll have to let me know, and we'll both have to make other arrangements. Now, though, I need to get back to work."

Not pausing to see or hear his reaction, Molly slipped into her low heels, ran a hand through her hair, and practically sprinted through the side door into the garage. Outside, she breathed a sigh of relief. She hoped he took seriously what she'd said. She hoped she would, too.

Returning home promptly at six, Molly said little, and Cooper said less. He relayed the details of Alec's adventure with the dog across the street and Emma's near-fall down the steps in Molly's pumps, saved only by Cooper's provident grab from behind at the top of the stairs. The twins, ravenous for dinner, were oblivious to the coolness in the air. Quickly exchanging goodbyes, Cooper headed to the front door as Molly reminded him of a couple details for the next day.

The rest of the week passed in a blur, each day like the one before, with no break in the strained moments between Cooper and Molly. Even the twins noticed, and Cooper often caught them with their little heads together, whispering, with occasional snatches of words floating out to Cooper's ears. He finally gave up trying to piece together what the two might be plotting. Dealing with the tension with Molly was hard enough.

All Friday afternoon, Emma distracted Cooper with her childish prattle, until his eyes glazed over and his head began to swim. Alec, less talkative but more prone to doing damage to himself or Cooper, finally interrupted her.

"Cooper, did my mommy remember to tell you that she, uh, she . . . she . . ." Looking over at Emma, who nodded encouragement, Alec tried valiantly to remember his lines.

"She what, Alec? What was she supposed to tell me?" It didn't surprise Cooper that Molly forgot to tell him something, since she kept her words to a minimum these days. Cooper would've wanted that only last week, when Molly always seemed to be giving orders. Now he hoped she'd break the silence. It was up to her.

After several nudges from Emma, Alec finally waved his hand at her, then turned back to Cooper. "She wanted you to stay with us tomorrow. I think she has to work. Or something. I forget."

"Oh. Geez. I wish she'd mentioned it earlier. I promised my mom I would — oh, hell — uh, I mean, heck. Okay. Yeah, I didn't want to do the rounds of Wayzata anyway. Best excuse in the world." Cooper frowned, trying to figure out how to tell his mother that he couldn't chauffeur her to the beauty parlor and shops tomorrow. She'd never believe he had a legitimate excuse. He'd used up too many phony ones over the years.

Minutes later, having lucked out when he got Clare Meredith's answering machine rather than the woman herself, Cooper pressed "end" on his cell phone just as Molly's house phone rang.

"Cooper!" Molly, in full-on frantic business mode, rattled into the phone. "Listen. I am so sorry, but I'm caught in the middle of some ugly stuff. We're trying to figure out what went wrong with all the numbers, all the orders. Everything is fouled up. My boss is screaming at me, and I'm in a bind.

Is there any way you could stay two or three hours late tonight?" Pausing only for a moment, she went on. "I totally understand if you can't. I could call Nancy or something."

"No, no prob. I didn't have any plans. I can stay as long as you need, so don't worry about it. I'll see you whenever." Cooper wondered what could cause an emergency late on a Friday, when most people had already left for the weekend, but he didn't question Molly. Her frenzy was obvious, as was her desperation.

"Thanks. Really. Gotta go."

Since he already knew Molly needed to work tomorrow, Cooper wondered a moment longer why the problem, whatever it was, couldn't be resolved then. The sound of a dial tone in his ear finally registered, leaving him to ponder it alone.

A little after nine o'clock, Cooper slouched on the living-room couch, the children safely in bed and he up to page six of his never-ending novel. Hearing the front door open, he looked up to see Molly trudge in, shoulders slumped.

"Hi." Attempting to wave, Molly barely managed a flick of her wrist.

"You look exhausted. Everything's fine, and no peeps from the dynamic duo. I guess

I should head out." Cooper closed his book and leaned forward, starting to stand up.

"No. I mean, sure, of course you can go. But I could use a drink, and I hate drinking alone. Especially tonight." Molly looked beaten, beyond exhaustion, as though she were more confused and upset than tired.

Cooper didn't need to be asked twice. He felt awful for Molly, knowing something terrible must've happened. He'd also been searching for an opening with her since that disastrous kiss on Monday. He'd settle for this.

"Absolutely. Here, sit down and put your feet up. I'll grab us something. What'll you have?" At Molly's direction, Cooper busied himself finding the bottle of scotch in the liquor cabinet, grabbing a couple of glasses and ice.

Returning to the living room, he saw Molly slumped in the middle of the patterned couch, and he opted for one end, sitting next to her, rather than in the plush armchair a few feet away. Reaching behind himself, he retrieved a throw pillow and, gently nudging Molly forward, placed it behind her head.

"Want to talk about it?" Cooper didn't want to pry, but Molly looked like she'd lost her best friend.

"I don't know. I'm not sure I even understand it well enough to tell anyone else." Letting her head fall back against the pillow, Molly closed her eyes. Cooper tried not to focus on her slender, exposed throat. Failing at that, he settled for keeping his lips and hands at a safe distance. Fists clenched, he vowed to listen passively, objectively, to whatever she told him.

"My boss — Jed — has been gone all week. Traveling on business, I guess, although I don't know where or why, since he and I normally bury ourselves in our offices for a couple weeks right after a New York trip." Molly shook her head, as if trying to make sense of everything.

Apparently, she couldn't. "Anyway, for whatever reason, he's been gone. Came back this afternoon, and within minutes he was ranting about this and that. If you cut through it, it was about sales numbers, mainly. Somehow it was my fault, even though I'm in charge of buying, not sales. I mean, they're connected, obviously, and I can't buy what won't sell, but . . ."

"Yeah, I understand. Sounds odd. So, what was it?"

Pausing to sip her scotch, Molly shook her head. "That's the thing. I still don't know. I went over everything, all the numbers, all the orders, all the sales records, this afternoon and evening. Something is wrong, but I can't figure it out. My assistant, Greta, couldn't either. We even called in a few of the number crunchers from upstairs, and someone from tech support, figuring it was either a numbers or computer glitch. No one could understand it. Then, right in the middle of it all, Jed disappeared. That was the last we saw of him."

Cooper's mind raced, frantically trying to fit the pieces together, wanting to solve Molly's dilemma. "So what's next? When will you see Jed? Are you going to have more number crunchers pore over the figures? Someone else? If you brought it home, I'll bet I could get to the heart of it before you know it."

Dazed, Molly looked at Cooper over the top of her glass. Knitting her brows together, both hands circling the glass, she just continued to sip.

Undeterred by her silence, Cooper continued to think aloud. "My guess is, the problem is with your computer." Nodding to himself, he snapped his fingers. "Yeah, I'm sure that's it. We had stuff like this happen all the time at my firm. No big deal. Usually just one little number is off, and there you go. All fixed. I bet it wouldn't take me more than fifteen minutes to find."

"Really." Molly carefully set her drink down on the coffee table and stretched her arms behind her head. She casually turned to face Cooper and spoke, an odd tone in her voice. "As easy as that."

Eager to prove his theory, Cooper heard the words but didn't understand their tone, not to mention the look on Molly's face. The exhaustion was now replaced by disbelief. Even though he knew what he was talking about. "Exactly. Anyway, we could fix it tomorrow morning. Maybe Nancy could stop by with her kids for an hour or so."

Molly's eyebrows went up as high as her forehead would allow. Standing, she crossed the room, turning off lights as she went. "You don't understand. I'm sure you *have* seen situations like this before, but so have all the people I brought in this afternoon and evening."

"I didn't mean it like —"

But he had, hadn't he? He clamped his mouth shut.

Molly shook her head at Cooper. "I didn't tell you about it so you could fix it. What you *did* for me tonight — staying with the kids — was a huge help, and I can't thank you enough. Right now, though, for once in my life, I just needed to unload on someone and talk it out. Not to get your legal advice, which I'm sure *is* perfectly brilliant — and I mean that — but to talk. The crazy thing is, a few minutes ago I also wanted your shoulder to lean on, maybe even to cry on, because I'm about ready to scream." She sighed, every inch of her drooping. "It probably sounds silly, I know. I really just needed a hug."

Her words, even though uttered softly and with the tenderness she usually reserved for her kids, were like a punch in the gut. The look on her face? Worse.

His entire career had been spent fixing people's problems, or at least making someone pay to fix them. It never occurred to him to offer anything less. But just to *be* there for someone? That issue, as Garrison would say, had never come up.

Cooper wanted to kick himself, or at least apologize and give her the belated hug she wanted. Too many years of legal training got in the way. Lawyers didn't admit they made mistakes. Even when the person with whom they had made the mistake was now looking at them with huge, tear-filled, gorgeous emerald eyes. Chagrin turned to embarrassment, and embarrassment to stoicism. "Sorry I wasn't what you wanted.

Guess I'll be going. See you at seven-thirty?"

Molly nodded and turned to walk up the stairs to her room. Cooper quietly let himself out.

He had a key, sure, but Cooper rang the doorbell promptly at seven-thirty the next morning, then waited, puzzled, hearing no answering thunder of footsteps from within. He knew for a painful fact, having been awakened at or before dawn by Emma and Alec, that the house was filled with early risers.

After a few minutes and a couple more unanswered rings, he debated his options. Leave and piss Molly off. Let himself in and possibly piss her off. Or Plan C. He walked around the side of the house and into the backyard.

There, Molly calmly, methodically, swam laps in the pool. The kids were nowhere in sight.

With her name on the tip of his tongue, Cooper stopped himself just before calling out a greeting. Still pissed at himself for being such an unfeeling know-it-all — such a *guy* — the night before, he didn't know how to approach Molly this morning. Didn't know what to say, despite spending half the night trying to figure out a solution to Molly's problem. Not that he'd ever admit it to her.

Cooper stared at her in silence, then wrestled with his tongue to force it to unscramble and say something intelligible. Even in a swimsuit obviously cut for serious swimming, not sunbathing, Molly was a vision. Long, sleek legs — made longer by the high cut of the fluorescent swimsuit — sliced through the water, and lithe arms arced effortlessly in tandem to create a textbook version of the crawl. The swimsuit molded to Molly's softly rounded bottom as she moved, with the deeply cut back skimming just below her waist.

If he drooled much more, there'd soon be a puddle the size of her swimming pool beneath him.

As that thought hovered in his mind, Molly gracefully somersaulted a racer's turn at the far end of the pool. As she twisted out of the turn and began the butterfly, Cooper knew the instant she spied him. Rather than rise for the next stroke, her arms flailed against the water and her head stayed under water a few extra seconds, leaving her sputtering when she stopped and stood up.

"What on earth are you doing here, Cooper?" Wiping the water out of her eyes with the back of her hand, Molly stared at Cooper as if in shock.

Struck dumb as he mentally traced the low neckline of Molly's swimsuit, Cooper recovered sufficiently to move his gaze higher. He met her eyes. Eyes that sparkled in the morning sun, shimmering against the reflection of the water.

Then he frowned. "What do you mean — what am I doing here? You said you needed me this morning. I mean, you needed me to watch the kids."

Molly blinked a few times before shaking her head. "What are you talking about? I never said that, and the kids aren't even here. They're over at Nancy's all day today. They got up at dawn to be ready in time for Nancy to pick them up. We've had this planned for a couple weeks."

Puzzled, Cooper squinted as he tried to ignore the water glistening on Molly's lightly tanned skin. "But . . . that can't be. They told me yesterday. Alec said you needed me to watch them today, then I forgot to confirm it with you when — when we, uh, talked last night."

Molly winced. "I guess I can see how that might've happened. But why would they say that? They've been so excited about going over to Nancy's, they just about burst every time I mentioned it this past week. Are you sure they weren't talking about some other time?"

Cooper wasn't mistaken about the day or time. He wasn't big on housework, but — thanks to his training as a lawyer — he was precise about time. Even when he ignored it.

He shook his head. "No, they definitely said today. I mean, I wouldn't have gotten that wrong. I feel pretty stupid now, showing up at the direction of a couple of four-year-olds, but I didn't think anything of it."

"A couple of devious little four-year-olds, it sounds like. I don't have the faintest idea what they were up to, but I'll get to the bottom of it." As she spoke, Molly moved to the side of the pool. In one clean movement, she placed her hands on the edge and sprang out of the water, twisting to land on her cute butt before continuing gracefully to a standing position. Grabbing a towel, she briskly rubbed her hair, then ran the towel down her arms and legs before wrapping it around her waist like a sarong.

Cooper wished he could think of an excuse to stay a little longer. Finally, he gave up. "I didn't mean to get them in trouble.

Anyway, I'll head out then. See you Monday?"

"Sure." Picking at an imaginary thread on her towel, Molly kept her head down. "Uh, you know, Cooper, if you didn't have anything else going on . . . I mean, I can't blame you if you say no, but I still haven't figured out what could've gone wrong at work, and, well, I guess two heads might be better than one. With a fresh look at everything, maybe you could see something I missed."

Of all the things he expected to come out of Molly's mouth, this had to be the last. Cooper's jaw dropped. "That's a joke, right? Look, I was an arrogant jerk last night, but I'd rather not go there again. I should stick to kid duty."

Molly looked at him, her embarrassment from last night and his reminder of it etched across her face. "Tell you what. I'll forget last night ever happened if you do. I was . . . disappointed, but I was also tired and frustrated. Like I said, you have every right to say no, but I would love your help. If you don't mind looking things over, I don't mind taking your advice. Even if you *are* a lawyer."

Seeing Molly wink as she threw out that last crack, Cooper laughed. He missed the mental challenges he got as a lawyer and didn't want to turn down the opportunity. He also didn't want to pass up an opportunity to work with Molly in a different setting. Some part of him realized that he wanted her to see him as more than just her kids' nanny. He'd *like* her to see him as a man. But this wouldn't be a bad start.

"Well, boss, you're on. You might want to throw on a few more clothes if you want me to have any hope of focusing on numbers, but . . ." Cooper grinned as he saw Molly blush. "Let's take a spin down to that office of yours and try to solve your problem. Together."

"Deal." Molly sashayed, much as Emma would have done, as she crossed the patio and went inside to change.

Too bad she didn't ask him to help her with *that.*

CHAPTER NINE

A long three hours later, Molly's head bent over the reams of computer printouts on her desk as Cooper paced her cramped office, hands clasped behind his head and eyes staring blindly at the ceiling tiles. Molly was right. Nothing added up.

Cooper's mind retraced the volumes of data that he and Molly had studied since arriving at her office, considering and rejecting theory after theory.

From what he could tell, there were no computer glitches, no mathematical errors. Either sales were grossly depressed over the prior year's, or something was seriously wrong for some other reason. That seemed more plausible. Merchandise buys were up over last year's and even slightly ahead of target, and inventory levels looked appropriate. It didn't make sense.

His own theory was probably grasping at straws. He'd seen something like this only once before, when he represented that huge beverage wholesaler in Iowa a couple years ago. They finally discovered that a crooked accountant dummied up the numbers to hide his artless attempt at embezzlement. With his embezzlement skills a solid match for his crappy accounting skills, it hadn't taken too long to draw out the truth.

This was different. Smelled different. Call it intuition, call it experience. It crossed too many departments, too many merchandise segments, for some low-level or even mid-level employee to carry out. It would almost take several employees, in different groups and with different areas of responsibility, to mess up the books this badly.

In Cooper's experience, it was rare that so many people could put something like this together without one of them folding under pressure.

The only other obvious possibility was that someone at a high level at Harrowby's was pulling this off, either single-handedly or with the help of one or two others. The culprit would almost have to be at or above Molly's level.

It wasn't Molly. She'd do something illegal the same day she'd let someone harm a hair on the heads of those two kids of hers. There weren't many other possibilities, though. At the very highest levels of management, ironically, they couldn't easily manipulate some of the numbers involved here, due to the amazing level of checks and balances that Harrowby's had in place.

Jed Parker, Molly's boss, seemed like a logical candidate from Cooper's viewpoint. Not necessarily the guilty party, but worth exploring. Molly shot down that idea, though, the minute Cooper ran it up the flagpole an hour ago. Called it ludicrous. Still . . .

"Hey, Moll. I know what you said, but I really think you should consider the possibility that your boss could be involved in this. At a minimum, if we analyzed the numbers from his perspective, we could either rule him out or figure out a new direction to take. We haven't tried that, you know. It's pretty standard on this stuff." Cooper stopped pacing as he spoke, looking at Molly for approval.

Molly glanced up quickly from the sales figures. "If it's standard, why haven't we done that analysis on me? Maybe I'm the bad guy here."

"No."

She shook her head. "If someone did this intentionally, Jed is the last person I'd suspect. Perfect life, perfect house, perfect everything. Comes from old money, and lots of it. What motive could he have? He's been a little strange lately, but that doesn't make him a criminal. I don't want to waste our time running down crazy ideas. We've already done enough of that as it is."

Absentmindedly chewing on her fingernail, Molly looked back down at the figures on her desk.

"I — oh, hell. You're probably right." Cooper didn't actually think that; Molly might be too close to the situation to view it clearly. But his theory was a long shot, and they both needed a break. For now, he wouldn't pursue this angle. He wouldn't mind avoiding another argument with Molly, either. He was still smarting from last night.

Molly continued to pore over the computer printouts. Her ability to focus rivaled his own, and he admired it. He also didn't mind having an excuse to stare at her. "So . . . got any ideas of your own? What's so interesting?"

"Oh, nothing I can put my finger on. Maybe it's time we took a break. I have numbers spinning around in my brain from looking at this so long." Molly looked up, languidly stretching her arms over her head as she smiled shyly at Cooper. Dusky creases of fatigue showed under her eyes.

"Sounds good to me. How about taking a spin around the lakes in my convertible? With the top down, you're guaranteed to shake those numbers loose." Cooper grinned at the thought of Molly with the wind rushing through her hair, sun dappling her cheeks.

Despite her complaints, Molly again studied the rows and columns staring back at her. "Oh. Geez. Wonderful offer, but I just thought of something I might've missed. Why don't you go without me? No reason for both of us to ruin a Saturday, and I already feel horribly guilty for wrecking so much of yours." When Cooper started to object, she waved at him, shooing him away with a smile. "No, really. You've helped me focus my search, even though nothing has come of it yet. But enough's enough. This isn't your problem, and I hate to waste your time."

"No waste at all. This is what I . . ." Trailing off, Cooper realized that he was about to tell his boss, for whom he was a nanny, that he did this. He felt a moment's regret that it wasn't true. The puzzles, the brainteasers . . . they'd always attracted him to law. Challenges like the one Molly was working so hard to solve. One she'd probably solve without any more help from him.

Absorbed in what she was reviewing, Molly hadn't heard Cooper's words. Just as well. Leaning over her desk, Cooper planted a kiss on the middle of her forehead, tucked a stray hair behind her ear. Startled, Molly looked at him quizzically.

"A kiss for luck, Moll. You can do it. I'll see you Monday morning."

Absorbed in what she was doing, Molly finally realized minutes later that she'd just sent Cooper away. On a sparkling Saturday, when she was starving for lunch — or something — and the kids were out of sight. Idiot. "Uh, thanks, Cooper," she called out to the now-empty hallway. She heard in response only the faint answering echo of his footsteps, then the sound of elevator doors closing.

Monday morning dawned bright and clear, but with a lingering chill in the air from last night's thunderstorm. Politely, Cooper rang the doorbell, not letting himself in with the key Molly gave him on his first day.

" 'Morning," he offered when she answered the door. Her hair and clothes crisply in place, she looked all business.

"Hi." Looking up, Molly smiled, perhaps

a little too brightly. "Thanks again for helping me out on Saturday. I still haven't been able to pull it together, but I must be getting close."

"No problem. Wish I could've done more. Any time you want more help on it, just ask." Cooper ruefully recalled having spent the remainder of the weekend wishing she'd done that. Ask. Invite him into her world.

Jake probably wouldn't invite him to another ball game anytime soon, he figured, after spending half the game Saturday night asking a nonresponsive Cooper what was up. Cooper couldn't explain, or even sort through in his mind, his mixed feelings. Molly. Being a lawyer. Being a nanny, for God's sake.

Cooper could tell that Jake was concerned, and he didn't relish the interrogation Jake was perfectly capable of giving him. Oddly, Jake finally left him alone. Always one to make the best of a situation, Jake spent the second half of the game chatting up the woman on the other side of him, eventually leaving with her. Some things never changed.

Molly made one final pass around the first floor, dropping kisses on the twins' foreheads while deftly avoiding their sticky fingers. Distracted, or just ignoring him —

Cooper couldn't tell which — Molly didn't seem to register his offer. She sure didn't take him up on it. "Looks like everything's okay around here. I don't expect to be late tonight, so see you at six, okay?"

Without waiting for a response, she walked out, letting the door close softly behind her.

As if he could look through it, Cooper stared pensively at the closed door. Not for long. With a belated cry to signal their advance, his two high-energy charges swooped down, clutching at his knees. Not for the first time, Cooper regretted his lack of armor. Or, at least, knee braces.

"Okay, guys. What's up today? Wrestling?" Offering a cry of his own, Cooper pivoted and simultaneously stooped to bring his head to their level, grabbing both twins in his arms before carefully rolling onto his back, taking them with him.

Shrieking, Alec tried twisting Cooper's arm while Emma tickled his stomach. With a clean backward somersault, to the amazement and thrill of the kids, Cooper disengaged himself from them and rolled to a standing position, only slightly out of breath. "Ha. You guys'll have to work a lot harder than that to take me down."

With that quick conclusion to their daily wrestling match, which Cooper only occasionally let the twins win, the trio launched into another day of frenetic activity. His lingering doubts about work forcibly pushed to the side, Cooper played to the twins' content. And to his own.

"Molly? Got a minute?" Greta Marshall, Molly's trusted assistant, poked her head in the door of her office, where Molly studied sales figures, her normal responsibilities sidelined until she could get her arms around the mess Jed insisted she was in.

Distracted, and despite her mood, Molly gave a welcoming smile. With a solution nowhere in sight, she might soon have all the time in the world. Even though this mess wasn't her fault, Jed didn't seem to agree. "Sure. What's going on? Find anything?"

Greta released a breath, inadvertently blowing her bangs into the air. "Not really. Some authorization codes aren't showing up, or are showing up more than they should, and I have Patrick checking on them. Otherwise, I can't see so much as a stray comma. What about you?"

Molly's mind flew to her initial, ugly meeting with Cooper, after the "stray" comma on his application gave him a foot in the door that he otherwise would've never gotten. Cooper. She was strongly attracted — something she hadn't experienced since Drew — and, more alarmingly, was starting to like him. She still couldn't understand why he'd leave a successful career for one as her nanny. Misgivings aside, though, she couldn't get him out of her mind. Or know what to say or do around him. Or know how to feel.

For so long now, a man had been the last thing on her mind. With the troubles at work, that should still be the case.

She ran a hand through her hair. "Probably nothing. I didn't even think to ask for it, but Riley ran a report on after-hours use of access cards on our floor for the past couple months. I saw Jed's number a little more than usual, but at times that made sense. Another number, too, at odd times. I don't recognize the number, but it doesn't say much. Think we should check it out?"

With all the numbers on the reports starting to make her go stir-crazy, if not brain-dead, Molly looked quizzically at her assistant, wishing Greta somehow knew the answer to the mystery or could at least take it off Molly's hands.

Reaching for the access report, Greta traced a polished fingernail down row after row. "Hmmm. Nothing rings a bell. Sure,

I'll check it out. If nothing else, it gives me an excuse to pay a visit to Riley." Batting her eyelashes, Greta gave an impish grin and sailed out the door.

Riley Burke, a new member of Harrowby's internal security detail, had already drawn buzz in the office for his roguish charm and chiseled good looks. Greta wasn't the only woman eager to check him out.

Laughing, Molly gave Greta the "okay" signal with her thumb and forefinger as Greta glanced back over her shoulder, already in pursuit of her quarry. Not to mention the mystery numbers.

She picked up her phone and hit the speed-dial button for home, surprised — and she told herself she was pleased, not disappointed — when Emma answered rather than Cooper. The kids were working on their telephone-answering skills, with predictably mixed results.

"Hi, sweetheart. How are you? Having fun?" Molly knew not to ask Emma what she had done so far today, having had to cut Emma off after ten minutes of nonstop narrative the last time she'd done so.

Emma giggled. "Oh, Mommy, we're having *so* much fun. Cooper splashed me and got me all wet, but I was in my swimsuit so that was okay, wasn't it, Mommy? Wasn't it? But then Alec splashed me too, and laughed, and then I didn't like it so much, so I got out of the pool, but I wasn't mad, but Alec thought I was, so he splashed me some more, and that wasn't very nice, was it? So I splashed him back, and Cooper helped me, and Brooke came over and helped, too. Isn't that funny, Mommy?"

Pausing for breath, Emma was blissfully unaware of Molly's own sudden intake of air and continued with her adventures. "I thought Brooke was going to get wet, too, but she had on a swimsuit, so I guess that was okay, huh, Mommy? But she didn't get wet, and then Cooper talked to her, and she went away again, but maybe she'll come back some more this afternoon, 'cause she likes Cooper, and she even likes me and Alec now and talks to us and stuff, so it's okay to talk to her, isn't it, Mommy? Or is she a stranger, so we aren't supposed to talk to her? I forget."

"No. Yes. Uh, I mean, yes, it's okay to talk to her, because she's our neighbor, Emma. But you probably ought to let me know when you talk to anyone other than Cooper, okay, honey? Just to be safe."

Knowing Emma, Molly guessed that the silence on the other end of the line signaled

Emma's nodding her head. She hadn't discovered yet that nodding or shaking her head wasn't transmitted over the phone line. "So . . . does Brooke come over often, Emma?"

"Yes, Mommy. Lots and lots. But I don't know why, 'cause she doesn't like to play in the tree house, or throw me the ball, or catch Alec's bugs, but I think bugs are icky, too, don't you?"

Before Molly could answer, or even form a thought that didn't involve flinging daggers at Brooke, Molly heard the phone clatter on what sounded like the brick patio by her pool. A few moments later, Cooper came on the line.

"Molly? Sorry I didn't pick up the phone sooner, but it's hard to commandeer it when Emma grabs it first." Did she imagine it, or did Cooper sound slightly out of breath? Inwardly kicking herself, Molly gathered her composure for a conversation that she'd eagerly, and foolishly, anticipated. Anticipated, that is, until Emma described Brooke's frequent presence in her yard — and maybe elsewhere in her home?

Absently, Molly twisted strands of her hair around her finger, ever tighter. Ignoring Cooper, she continued to puzzle over Brooke. Why were men so quick to ignore her and to move on to someone new? What did she lack? And why did she have the bad luck to live next door to Brooke?

Only when the hair now gripped savagely in her fingers began to pull away from her scalp, making her wince, did Molly become aware that Cooper was repeating her name. He'd probably done so several times already, and it only now registered on her brain.

"Oh . . . hi, Cooper. Sorry to keep you waiting. Someone came into my office right after Emma dropped the phone." At this point, Molly didn't care about hurting Cooper's feelings or leaving him dangling, but her ingrained politeness made her utter the excuses she heard come out of her mouth.

"No problem." Cooper didn't seem to care. As usual. "What's up? You don't usually call during the day. Need to work late again tonight?"

"Uh, no. I had a spare moment and just wanted to check in on the kids. Sorry to bother you. I'll let you go." Molly hung up the phone without bothering to exchange the usual courtesies, even the shortest "bye." For a moment, she was glad to have the problem with the sales figures. It might distract her from the kick in the teeth she'd just received.

Cooper stared at the phone in his hand, the dial tone still humming after Molly's abrupt end to the call. What was that about? It didn't seem like Molly at all — at least, not the Molly he'd lately begun to glimpse.

Everyone around here was getting strange. Amending himself, he noted that the kids were still great. But maybe weirdness would start sneaking up on them, draw them into its spell by the time they were, say, six.

Molly blew hot and cold. A couple kisses, alternating with bouts of the deep freeze. If she'd stayed on the line another few minutes, he had a feeling that arctic air would have blasted through the telephone straight at him. No telling why, but somehow he must've managed to annoy her again. He was good at that. A real talent.

Then there was Brooke. Here, there, everywhere. Every time he turned around, she popped up. And, generally, popped out. Of her swimsuit, her halter tops, micro miniskirts, you name it. Whatever she wore was always a whole lot of nothing.

Cooper wished that Jake had taken him up on his idle offer to set him up with Brooke. He shouldn't do it to his friend, but Jake was the kind of guy who could enjoy an evening with someone like Brooke and move on to someone else the next day without a backward glance. Cooper had never mastered that trick. He didn't want to start now.

And Nancy. Now that her kids had weathered the chicken pox with a minimum of fuss, she called or stopped by when she had a chance. Nancy was strange, too, but only with that babbling thing of hers. Man, could she talk. On the other hand, she was up front — except when Molly had been in New York — and refreshingly candid about the way things were with Molly and everything else. She even bailed him out, now and then, when he screwed something up royally. Like confusing bleach for laundry detergent. Nancy was, to put it bluntly, his lifeline. Without her he'd be toast.

Cooper had left a world where he'd mostly been surrounded by men. Except for Alec, he was surrounded by women now. No problem there. But why did one have to babble him senseless, one chase him into the ground, and one have to be Molly?

Shrugging, he gave up his analysis, which was something best left at his old law firm. It didn't do him a bit of good around here.

■ ■ ■ ■

Earlier promises to the contrary, Molly called Cooper back later that afternoon, crossing her fingers as she told him she might have a possible breakthrough in her work problems. As she held her breath, he immediately offered to work longer that night.

Slumped over her desk, Molly felt only defeat. There was no breakthrough. Glimmers of hope kept springing up, only to be pounded into submission by a new set of facts, always contradicting the earlier ones. Molly had never seen anything like it. At least fifteen people — with that number rising steadily — were now devoting untold hours to the issue, mostly as a favor to Molly. She was grateful. She'd be even more grateful for an actual solution.

The numbers didn't make her look good. In fact, she'd be pretty suspicious if she were any of the other fifteen people looking at it. Luckily, her efforts for Harrowby's over the years, and all the little favors she'd done for people, made the difference. Loyalty still counted for something, at least among her immediate coworkers. Only Jed was alternately yelling at her or lying low.

Molly's mind drifted back to Cooper. And Brooke. It disgusted Molly even to think about Brooke, to have to think about her. It was crazy, she knew, but Molly almost felt like the two of them had crept into her home when she wasn't looking and robbed her blind. Not the cars, not the furniture, not the clothes or jewelry or what-have-you. Just Molly's life. Her kids were so thrilled with Cooper, she was almost starting to feel invisible at home. Why bother going there? And if she did, would she just interrupt a tryst between Brooke and Cooper?

Shuddering, she closed her eyes and breathed in and out, slowly, feeling the pain skitter across her chest as her heart broke into a million pieces. Objectively, she knew she hadn't tried with Cooper. She'd kept him at arm's length because she didn't want to fail again with another man. Her ego insisted, ridiculously, that she just didn't want to lose a nanny.

Okay, *that* made her laugh, even if the laugh was hollow. Cooper Meredith was a world-class lawyer taking a summer break. Sure, the guy would never be much of a nanny, but he had everything else going for him. Qualities that put him in a completely different league from Drew and almost any other guy Molly had ever known.

Her heart wanted him. So did the rest of her.

Would he ever see it? And if he did, would it make any difference?

CHAPTER TEN

Cooper talked Emma and Alec into an early bedtime. Not early by Molly's pristine standards — okay, so maybe it was nine o'clock instead of eight — but at least an hour earlier than the ten o'clock they wanted and, with him, usually got.

At ten after nine, he changed into his now-dry swimsuit — hours after the impromptu game of let's-dunk-Cooper the twins invented that afternoon — and executed a clean dive into the pool, slicing through the water and enjoying the respite from the lifeguard duty that most of his pool time entailed.

Molly had been a little vague about when she'd get home. It didn't matter much to him, but he could see the difference in the twins when they didn't get as much attention from her as usual. Cooper was their pal, their buddy, but Molly was their mom. Hands down, she was top of the pile with them. Tonight they'd been dragging, a little glum at dinner, and didn't tease each other as much as usual.

He hoped Molly fixed the problem at work soon. For her sake. For the sake of her kids, so they could all enjoy the rest of the summer. And maybe, just maybe, so he could see if there might be anything left of her for him.

Finishing a brisk twenty laps, Cooper turned and floated idly on his back, gazing up at the stars poking through the inky sky beyond the trees overhead. Lost in a reverie of imagined beginnings with Molly, he never heard Molly's footsteps as they approached, only belatedly saw that the subject of his thoughts stood at the side of the pool, staring at him with a mixture of fascination and . . . hurt?

The fascination part, he liked. The hurt? He must be mistaken about that.

Smoothly arcing into a side roll as he turned toward Molly and dove under water for the last few yards, Cooper shot back to the surface, popping into the air before gliding over to the edge of the pool. He propped his chin on his folded arms. From his vantage point, he looked up and had a clear view of . . . not much, since it took only a startled moment before Molly backed up a few feet from the edge.

"Hey, Moll. Looks like you're holding up pretty well. Any good news on the work front?" Involuntarily, Cooper's eyes raked Molly as he spoke. *Holding up pretty well* was the understatement of the year. The woman was pulled together, totally, twenty-four hours a day, no question. He tried to imagine her with her hair mussed, her clothes askew. The thought brought an involuntary shudder, followed immediately by a surge of arousal. Cooper's embarrassment, even though he knew Molly couldn't see him, matched his fascination at having achieved that feat in the chilly water.

Molly started to answer, then apparently thought better of it. She clamped her lips together and stared, puzzled, at Cooper. Maybe she couldn't see beneath the edge of the pool, but from the look on her face, she must have read something in his eyes to make her pause. Belatedly, Cooper blanked his facial expression.

Molly's gaze took in the length of the pool. "No, nothing much. More of the same." Moving closer to the edge of the pool, Molly twirled her finger in her hair as she looked at Cooper, then looked away, repeating the motion a few times. "Um, were you planning on swimming much longer? I could, you know, change into a swimsuit and . . . join you. I mean, if you weren't done or something."

Cooper marveled at Molly's difficulty in stringing together her words. It rivaled his speaking ability the first day he met her. He was also in no hurry to leave the pool in his current condition, which showed no sign of fading. "That'd be great. I was just doing some laps."

Molly didn't wait to hear more. Spinning on her heel, she started toward the sliding-glass door into the house.

"Uh, Molly?" Her footsteps stilled, but she didn't turn around again to look at him. "No need to change into a swimsuit on my account. I won't tell." Not wanting to hear her sputtered reply, Cooper dove sideways into the water, coming back up to the surface a minute later with Molly no longer in sight. Grinning, he whistled tunelessly while he awaited her next appearance.

Cooper had said out loud the very thought she was musing — not seriously musing, but indulging herself in a little fantasy. Those fantasies were becoming a frequent visitor these days. Too bad they had to suffice, because she couldn't indulge in the real thing.

Molly yanked open her swimsuit drawer, then ransacked it to find something that wasn't completely utilitarian. Finally, bunched up in a tiny ball in the farthest corner of the drawer, she spied a string bikini she hadn't worn in a million years. Since before Alec and Emma.

Taking off her jewelry, followed by the silk shirtdress she'd worn to work, Molly stripped out of her lingerie and wiggled into the bikini. She gazed into the mirror, debating whether to change into a more practical swimsuit, like she usually wore, or maybe just call off the whole swimming thing. A glance at the clock told her she'd kept Cooper waiting too long.

Oh, hell. With a toss of her hair, she told herself Cooper wouldn't even notice what she wore. He'd practically dared her to go skinny-dipping, but the grin in his voice told her he was just kidding, probably trying to shake her up a little. Feeling a little sick, she went down the stairs slower than she'd gone up. May as well just go for a swim.

Cooper was back at the side of the pool when Molly returned, his chin propped in one hand. He must have finished his laps and was just waiting around to humor her. Worse yet, he probably thought he had to wait because she was his boss. Even though his nanny job was a whim, he took employment roles seriously. She wished she'd thought this through before asking him to swim with her.

At the sound of the sliding-glass door, Cooper's gaze shot straight to Molly. His jaw dropped as his eyebrows shot upward, and the hand on which he'd propped his chin flew out from his face, making a cracking sound as it struck the tile around the pool. Wincing, his eyes retreated from Molly, staring at the hand and wrist he now shook in pain.

Molly's eyes took in his visible reaction, but her heart and mind weren't fooled and searched for a reason for his apparent shock. Maybe the sound of the door startled him as his mind thought through . . . well, whatever it was thinking. Wasn't that what lawyers did all the time? Think? He probably couldn't shake that out of his system after only a few weeks away from his law firm.

The evening breeze whispered through the trees, reminding Molly with tiny goose bumps that she didn't have much on. She'd also forgotten to bring a towel or cover-up outside. She noticed a couple of towels on the chair on the far side of the pool, but the shortest distance from here to there was through the pool, so . . . no time like the present. Stepping to the edge, she plunged in.

Her dive took her across the pool, and she continued in that straight line rather than swim the length of the pool as she normally would. Pausing at the other side, she saw Cooper making his way to her. Before she could decide whether to swim back to the other side or to one end, he was beside her. Close beside her.

Arms around her waist, face-to-face, holding her in his arms.

Molly's head dropped back as she stared into his eyes. Her fantasies hadn't been this . . . real. Before she could run a play-by-play comparison, though, his lips pressed against hers, claiming her. The water did nothing to tamp the flames leaping between them, sizzling the air around them.

Lost, Molly surrendered to Cooper's embrace, her questions — about the propriety, the *sense* of this — fading like a whisper stolen by the wind. Her lips met his, seeking more than mere pleasure. Captivated, Molly wound her arms around Cooper's neck, drawing him closer to her. She heard only the frantic pounding of her heart.

Cooper's lips moved to her earlobe, teasing it before pressing a soft kiss on her forehead, then the tip of her nose. Molly felt her knees start to buckle, her body press against his. Cooper's arms wrapped around her, holding her against him, leaving her hands free to tangle themselves in his hair as their lips pressed together.

As Molly felt herself losing the last of her grip on sanity or self-control, her hands found his chest, tracing a swirling pattern there before moving lower, to his waist. Before she knew what was happening, Cooper took her gently by the wrist.

"Moll, let's . . . take our time." Cooper's words were replaced by sudden movement as he grabbed her by the waist, lifting her out of the water to set her on the pool's edge.

"There. Perfect." Cooper quit talking, blessedly. He wrapped both arms around her waist, and Molly's legs wrapped themselves around him, drawing him closer.

Cooper drew a ragged breath. "Folly. *Molly*, I —"

Whatever he'd been about to say was lost in the shrill ringing of the portable phone two feet away from Molly. *No.* Why was the phone out here, when it should've been inside where she wouldn't have heard it? She wanted this moment with Cooper. She wanted him. She wanted to explore the possibility of *them*.

Molly tried to ignore the ringing. She also tried to ignore the fact that Cooper had called her Folly a couple times now — what did that mean? Was Folly some bizarre pet nickname for some other woman? Was it his pet nickname for *her*? — but Cooper was already moving away from her. Whether it was the cool breeze or the abandonment that chilled her, she didn't know. Grabbing a towel as she picked up the handset, Molly managed only a brusque hello.

Molly's bubbly assistant, Greta, chirped into the phone, unaware of her untimely interruption. "Molly? That *is* you, isn't it? Are you there?"

Greta was nothing if not persistent. No point in hanging up. She would just call back or, worse, drive over in her car. She lived only a mile away and would think nothing of it.

"I'm here. Sorry. Guess I was . . . distracted. What were you saying?" Embarrassed, Molly heard the breathlessness in her own voice and struggled to sound like herself again: the calm, cool, collected woman Greta and everyone else knew and expected. Not the woman who, a moment ago, had been tangled in Cooper's arms, wanting him, hoping he wanted her every bit as much.

Greta was unfazed and obviously ignorant of anything special going on. "Sounds like you're tied up, but I couldn't wait until tomorrow to tell you."

"Tell me what?" Molly was eager to return to Cooper's arms, but something in Greta's voice piqued her curiosity.

The sound of chewing gum crackled over the phone. "I think we've finally got something."

Molly's mind reeled at the possibility of an end to the puzzle. "Do I need to come back down to the office tonight?" Molly saw the frown on Cooper's face as she spoke the words. Horrible timing, yes — the worst — but she knew this had to be a priority.

Story of her life.

Greta cleared her throat. "Uh, no. No need to come down, but we might actually have a breakthrough. Sorry to call so late. I just wanted to let you know right away."

With the click of Greta's hang-up all she could respond to, Molly set the phone on the nearest chair. Shaking her head, she pulled the towel tighter around herself and looked at Cooper, now sitting on the edge of the pool.

"That was my assistant. She thinks we

might have a breakthrough, but we'll know more in the morning."

Cooper rose and walked a couple steps toward Molly, stopping when he saw her take a step back. She shivered, lost in thought.

"That's great, Moll. Tomorrow, huh? But what about tonight? Am I wrong, or are you not interested anymore?"

The breeze wasn't making Molly shiver. The embarrassment of being in a swimsuit with Cooper a few moments ago, being touched . . . held . . . kissed out of her mind. Ready to beg him for more. Wow. She hadn't felt that way in forever.

Molly felt herself blushing furiously and looked away. She wanted Cooper. She just didn't know what to do about it. "I — I don't know right now. I'm sorry if I —"

Cooper closed the short distance between them. Swept her into his arms, crushed her against him. Tilting her chin up to force her to look at him, he spoke, more softly than the anger in his eyes suggested. "Sorry? What are you talking about? I could have sworn there were two of us in that pool — two adults — who both wanted what was happening. Was I mistaken?"

"No." Molly pressed gently against his chest to gain some breathing room. Some distance. A chance to think. "I'm not play-ing games. I'm not too good at it, even if I tried."

Cooper's eyes clouded over with some-thing that looked like hurt.

"Look, I'm sorry, Cooper. Really sorry. I'm not sure what's going on or exactly what either of us wants, and I'm too tired to figure it out tonight. But I'd like to. Soon. Could we talk about this tomorrow? If you still want to?"

Clutching her towel tightly around herself, Molly knew she must look and sound like an idiot. It explained the range of expres-sions taking turns on Cooper's face and in his eyes. "Whenever you want. But no mat-ter what you wanted tonight, make no mistake about what I wanted. I wanted you. All of you. I still do."

Abruptly, he spun and dove into the pool, coming up for air only when he reached the other side. With both hands firmly grasping the edge, he pulled himself out in one clean move. Molly stared at the water glistening on his back, dripping from his swimsuit.

"Cooper?" She waited as he turned to face her across the width of the pool. "For the record, I wanted you tonight, too. I just need to think."

For a moment, Cooper said nothing, just

tilted his head to one side as he studied her intently. Too intently. "Goodnight, Moll. See you tomorrow."

The next morning, Molly's head was still spinning. Coffee, Tylenol, even a triple-berry scone — her surefire cures for almost anything — failed her. She barely looked up when Greta showed up in her office, grinning like a cat.

"I take it you have good news. Does it have anything to do with the numbers, or did Riley have success with something else, too?"

Greta laid a stack of papers on Molly's desk, squaring them neatly in front of Molly. She took a step back, crossed her arms, and paused for dramatic effect.

"Ask Jed. Looks like he and his precious bimbo have been up to a little something. Or a big something. Big dollars. And you know what else? They wanted to make you pay for it."

CHAPTER ELEVEN

"What are you talking about? Jed? I don't understand." Molly's mind raced through the possibilities. Was Greta mistaken? She had to be mistaken. By now it was clear to everyone — no, strike that. The suits upstairs might not have seen, or heard, what the people in the buying group had been buzzing about for at least a couple of weeks now. That Jed had been acting strange.

Even so, it didn't make him a thief.

Greta sighed, loudly, and rolled her eyes. "As if! Like there's anything in the world you don't get, Molly."

Molly could think of at least one thing, but she didn't need to get into the details of how wrong Greta happened to be. "No, really, Greta. What is it? I can't imagine what Jed could've done. To me?"

When Greta searched Molly's face, frowning, Molly shivered. How bad *was* it?

"It's like this. We finally found a pattern

in what was happening, but it was pretty late when we did, and Riley and I were half dead on our feet. We decided to regroup today and look at this again, but there's something there. It seems to point to Jed, but it points to you, too, Molly."

Molly couldn't believe her ears. Even Greta suspected her? "Greta! You can't be — I never —"

"No! That's not what I meant. Of course you didn't do anything. It doesn't take half a brain to know that. But that's what made it so obvious, see? Since we knew you couldn't have done it, we looked past the apparent patterns in the spreadsheets and were able to see something else. And what we saw was Jed."

Molly looked down at the papers on her desk, squinting to make sense of the same rows and columns she'd stared at for the past couple weeks. No luck. She didn't have a clue what patterns Greta meant. "What do you mean, you saw Jed? Where?"

Greta walked around Molly's desk, stopping behind her, then leaned down to look over her shoulder. "There." She pointed with a hot-pink lacquered nail to the third column, a couple inches from the top of the first page. "Number 7399919 is all over the printouts."

Molly stared at the number, which indeed repeated itself throughout that page and, from her quick shuffle through the stack of papers, basically everywhere. The computer run covered the last month and was filled with the mystery number. Perusing the columns more closely, Molly saw a noticeable gap during the period she'd been in New York.

But what did it mean? "It looks like number 7399919 must've traveled to New York with me, since it vanished off the page when I went there."

"You're quick, Molly. I've gotta give you that."

Quick? About *what*? The hard knot in the pit of Molly's stomach told her she wasn't sure how much she wanted to know, but she'd postponed the inevitable long enough. "What do you mean, I'm quick? I was joking!"

Okay, half joking.

Greta blew out a breath, then stepped to the side of Molly's desk, shuffling through the stack of papers until she got to the ones dated the week of the New York trip. "Like I said, we still need to cross-check this against some other records. But, basically, the week you were in New York made Riley realize what happened."

It didn't take much to see that Greta's eyes shone more brightly when she mentioned Riley's name. If he got Molly out of a mess, Riley would be high on her own hit parade, too.

"See, that column lists the authorization code for each transaction by everyone's user number. We noticed the mystery number all over the place. At first I figured it didn't mean much, because it's a temporary number — not assigned to anybody, just what we would use for a day or so whenever a new employee starts. Riley asked if we had a bunch of new people lately. When I said no, he ran all these numbers through the computer. He's a total genius."

Molly still didn't see where this was heading. The sick feeling in the pit of her stomach alternately eased or grew worse as the details flooded past her.

"Agreed. Riley is a genius. I still don't understand what this means, though, or why it affects *me.*" Tamping down her impatience, Molly tried to let Greta get to the end of the story without shrieking and tearing out her hair, both of which were tempting.

Greta tapped her nail on the top sheet of paper. "The mystery number is a temporary number used for new employees under *you.*

Jed has one, too, like all the top guys. You don't use it, but the people you're responsible for use it. It's a control thing. Anyway, we figure Jed is the one using it, or letting his babe or someone else use it. I don't know why, but they're setting you up. Hey, I gotta run. I'll tell you more later."

Greta grabbed the sheaf of papers on Molly's desk and shot out the door. Molly was left with no papers to study and an explanation with a lot of holes. She still didn't see what Jed could possibly have to do with all this, or why he would dump on her in any case. Despite a bundle of papers filled with columns of numbers, nothing added up.

"I've got to get out of here." Rising to her feet, Molly didn't realize the backs of her legs had slammed into her chair until it fell over backward, crashing against the floor. Her hands trembled and felt clammy. Squeezing her fingers into tight fists, she extended them, staring almost mechanically at her fingers as she flexed each of them. Rotated her wrists. Raised and lowered her shoulders. Tilted her head backward, forward, then in a slow circle.

Tension hummed through her, unrelieved by her impromptu calisthenics. Another couple minutes of this, and someone would poke his head in the door and ask her if she was joining a gymnastics team. Or Jed would come by. What could she say to him? Not much. Until Greta and Riley finished doing whatever they were doing, she didn't understand a single thing and couldn't articulate an accusation, much less a compelling one.

Whirling, Molly took a look around her office. She'd spent too many years, days, and hours here, backbreaking ones, to be set up as someone's sucker. Her calm side, which normally dominated, had to wait for the answers so she could make sense out of this muddle. The part of her brain that controlled her legs wanted to get out of here. Now.

Heels clattering against the floor at the speed of sound, Molly followed her assistant's lead and shot out of the office. Unlike Greta, she was headed home.

"Hi, Emma and Alec. Guess what? I'm home early!" Despite her throbbing headache, Molly put on a good front for the kids. They didn't deserve to get hit with her real mood, which was past angry and fast on its way to bone-deep depression.

Besides, didn't they always cheer her up? She could use that right now.

Desperately.

Emma barely looked up from the Play-Doh monstrosity she was building on the kitchen table. Alec didn't do even that. Feet curled around the legs of one of the living-room chairs, he lay on his stomach, intently sorting through the pieces of a puzzle.

"Hi, Mommy." Emma flickered a small smile at Molly before resuming work on her masterpiece.

After the morning she'd had, Molly didn't appreciate the underwhelming reaction she received. Were the kids sick? What happened to her loving but boisterous little imps?

"Alec? You okay, sweetie?" Molly looked over at her little rogue, entranced in his puzzle. He still hadn't looked up. She walked into the living room and, bending down, playfully nudged his side with the toe of her shoe.

Alec absently rubbed his side before returning to his puzzle. "Yeah? Why did you come home?"

Alec's words, which sounded more like those of a teenager than a four-year-old, stung. Molly reminded herself he was only four. Moreover, he had no idea why, today of all days, she needed a heavy dose of childish love from her two little ones.

Where was Cooper? What had he done to her children?

As if her thoughts conjured him up out of thin air, Cooper strolled into the front hall from the back of the house, holding what looked like one of Alec's shirts. Or, at least, one that might once have been, now covered with mud and ripped in at least a couple places. "Alec, remember what I said about —"

Breaking off when he spotted Molly, Cooper affected a belated look of nonchalance as he tucked the shirt, now a rag, behind his back.

"Hey, Moll. What's up? Are you between appointments or something?"

Her children forgotten for the moment, Molly pointed at the arm that remained hidden behind his back. "Nice try. Using my kids' clothes for cleaning rags? If you want, I could show you where the dust cloths are."

Blanching, Cooper put his hands up as if in surrender. "You win, detective. The case of the runaway T-shirt is now solved."

Alec, who jumped to his feet at the sound of Cooper's voice, now ran to him and grabbed the shirt out of Cooper's hand. "Thanks, Coop! I like that one a lot."

With a wry look, Cooper snatched it back from him. "You mean, you *used* to like this one a lot. If your mom has anything to say about it, I think it's headed for the trash."

"What does she know? I *want* that shirt. Can't you make her let me keep it?" Alec jumped all around Cooper, who held the offending garment high over his head, out of reach. If Cooper had a reaction to Alec's outburst, he wasn't showing it.

It didn't matter. Molly's own reaction more than made up for any Cooper might have.

"*Make* me let you keep it, young man? Who's your mother, Alec? Who's in charge here?" Seeing Alec look quickly from Cooper to her and back again, Molly decided she didn't want to hear Alec's answer. For his sake, he'd better not say anything. "And before you answer that, I think you'd better spend some time in your room thinking good and hard about your answer. Now, march."

She didn't miss the look Cooper gave Alec as, before heading to his room, the boy's eyes pleaded for intervention from his male hero. Cooper clearly warned him off that tactic. Good. At least Cooper knew when a fuse was about to ignite.

Cooper wasn't completely successful, though. As Alec dragged one foot after the other down the hall, Molly could hear him muttering about his rotten mom. He was almost out of earshot when she caught the worst of his wailing. "Why'd she hafta come home? Cooper's fun. Mommy's a big meanie."

Molly winced. A child shrink would probably say he was asserting his independence, an important part of growth, or some such garbage. It felt more like a gratuitous slam. Sometimes, even a four-year-old could pack a wallop.

Trying to let it slide, and to regroup, Molly looked around. Emma still wasn't stirring from her Play-Doh. That meant Cooper was the only one paying attention to her. So much for getting relief from work.

"I won't ask what happened to that shirt. I don't think I want to know." On the verge of tears, Molly's voice caught. She couldn't bear more bad news, no matter how trifling.

Finally drawn out of the disaster she was making on the kitchen table, Emma skipped over to Molly, hugging her thighs. "Don't be sad, Mommy. Alec didn't mean to be bad. But why did you leave your big office? Cooper's taking good care of us, really. We're having lots of fun, and we're not doing anything Mommy wouldn't like, are we, Cooper? Huh, Cooper?"

"With the exception of a stray T-shirt, which I just retrieved from a branch above the tree house, we're all behaving ourselves admirably. Even I am. I assure you, madam, your rules were followed to the letter today."

At Molly's raised eyebrows, Cooper grinned sheepishly. "Okay, I admit the day is barely half over, and at least one of us would've gotten into some serious trouble before the day was out. But with you home now, we might not suffer that fate." Sweeping one arm wide in an exaggerated arc before bringing it back to his waist and bowing deeply, Cooper resumed his stance, much to Emma's delighted giggles and clapping.

"Oh, puh-lease." Molly laughed in spite of herself.

Cooper picked up Emma and, with her in his arms, again swooped low in a bow, this time taking Emma down with him. Her curls brushed the floor as she screeched in excitement.

"Anyway, what's up? What brings you home early? Good news at work?" Cooper obviously couldn't read anything in her face, or he wouldn't have asked. Molly couldn't remember the last time she'd had good news.

She didn't want to rehash what she didn't understand. She'd come home to get away from all that, even if only for a few hours. Home used to be her sanctuary from the travails of work, although she hadn't had many travails until recently. Now, with everything exploding at work and with Cooper in her home, her head never stopped spinning.

Rescuing Emma from Cooper's arms, Molly lifted her up, then wrapped her arms around her little girl and breathed deeply. Too deeply. Emma, who usually reeked of a mix of Molly's perfume bottles and bubble bath, now smelled like a bizarre conglomeration of Play-Doh, dirt, and paint. It explained the vivid slashes of red and yellow on her otherwise blue-green top.

So much for her formerly sweet-smelling little girl. Oh, well. It had probably been too good to last.

The sound of Cooper clearing his throat reminded Molly that she hadn't answered his question. His very appropriate question, since it was a rare day that Molly made it home on time, let alone early.

"Do you mind if I don't go into it?" At the hurt look that flickered over his face, she sighed. "It's work. We've had a possible breakthrough, but I'm not yet sure what it means, and it's not over. I came home to escape, even if just for a few hours. Is that asking too much?"

"You could ask a lot more of me. You

227

know that. When you want to admit it —
when you're ready to break down and *rely*
on someone other than yourself, you know
where to find me." Cooper jammed his fists
in his pockets and stalked over to the
sliding-glass door, letting himself outside
and into the backyard.

Cooper had had it up to *here* with Molly's
attitude. She hadn't been rude — not at all
— but she also couldn't ask anyone for help
and wouldn't accept it if offered. Hell, the
woman wouldn't let him save her if she were
in quicksand with a crocodile two feet away.
Stubborn.

She reminded him of himself.

Here he was, standing outside, with the
woman he wanted a mere fifteen feet away,
but separated from him by a glass door.
Might as well be the Great Wall, for all that
either of them would capitulate in the
other's direction.

He just wanted to help. Maybe it wasn't
all he wanted, but from a nonphysical
perspective, it was a lot of it. No, that wasn't
really true. He wasn't ready to admit it to
her or anyone else, but he missed the action. The thrill, the exhilaration of solving
some dilemma that had everyone else
twisted up in knots. The more knots, the

better. The more people he could outlast and outsmart, the happier he was.

A couple of little kids weren't much of a challenge to his intellect. Emma and Alec were great kids. Spunky, fearless, up for anything. And only four! Having each other for comrades must give them an edge. Otherwise, he couldn't imagine other kids that age able to come up with the stunts these two did.

He just didn't want to spend the rest of his life having his greatest challenge be how to get grape juice stains out of white shorts. Or how to amuse two rambunctious kids hours after his own batteries gave out. They were a handful, all right.

He also wanted Molly, but more than that? Hard to say. It seemed like enough for now. Getting her alone for a moment, without the kids and with the fire of lust rather than annoyance in her eyes, would be enough. And if that happened, *when* that happened, he'd have time enough to figure out whether something beyond *want* could become part of his vocabulary. Or part of hers.

Belatedly, with his back to the house, Cooper realized that the sliding-glass door had opened and Molly was right behind him. The tangy-floral scent she wore teased him, sharpening his awareness of her, and the assault on his senses left him fully alert. In more ways than one, he noted, as he glanced down at the burgeoning interest reflected on the front of his slacks. Great. It was going to be a little difficult hanging on to his anger when his body betrayed him so profoundly.

Without turning around, Cooper spoke first. "Where's Emma? Did you pack her off to her room, too? One by one, I'm losing all my supporting troops."

Molly didn't respond, figuring he wasn't expecting it. Emma had vanished to her room without any encouragement from Molly, saying she was sleepy. It stunned her, but she wasn't complaining.

Instead, she moved closer to Cooper, wrapped her arms around him, tightening them as she pressed against his back, one cheek rested gently against him. She sighed. He felt so good. So solid.

It might've been selfish of her to freeze him out of her bad day, but she needed a break, and talking about Jed and work weren't going to give her that anytime soon. It was also so hard — no, *difficult,* she thought as she smiled, since hardness conjured up something else altogether. So difficult to think of someone who played the role of her nanny as a confidante or advisor. Someone she could rely on.

That was the problem. Cooper was "playing the role" of her nanny. The guy might be great with kids, but he was no nanny. The brief time they'd spent working through her issues at the office proved it to her beyond doubt. Cooper was a lawyer at heart. An incredibly smart, talented, *perceptive* lawyer. He should be using the skills he'd acquired as a lawyer. Didn't he realize it?

"Hey." The low rumble of his voice interrupted her musings, but she hated to give up her impromptu afternoon snuggle. Even if she might prefer a horizontal one over the vertical.

"Hmmm?"

Cooper executed a slow spin, winding up still in her arms but with Molly now face-to-face with him. Or chest-to-chest.

"Funny, I never pictured you for the huggy type. I thought that was more Emma's style. Does she take after her mom after all?" As he spoke, Cooper ran one hand softly though her hair, rolling it in his fingers, while he let his other hand drift in a lazy circle on her back.

"She definitely takes after her mom. Her

mom just isn't quite so quick to make everyone aware of that little trait." Molly's eyes brightened at the tenderness of his hands, the gentle teasing of his words.

His laughter rumbled deep in his chest. "Quite so quick? If that isn't the understatement of the day, I don't know what is."

Blushing, Molly refused to relinquish her hold on him. "Hmmpf! As if . . ."

Cooper silenced her with a finger on her lips. "Hey, just teasing." He paused at her raised eyebrows. "Okay, I wasn't. You're not exactly one to spill your guts or show everything you think or feel. Believe me, that's not the worst sin in the world. As it happens, I've been accused of that failing myself."

"Oh? Care to elaborate?"

Tipping up her chin to look at him, Cooper grinned. "No. Not particularly."

Molly decided to give him his space. Figuratively, at least, since her body continued to melt into him. "That's what I expected."

"Listen, before I go getting all mushy, as Alec would say, and kiss you, could we talk? Unless you need more time to regroup, I'd like to hear what's going on."

Molly mulled his question as she inventoried her feelings. They kept changing. If anything was going to happen with Cooper — which might be either a good thing or a horrific thing, depending on her scattered thoughts — it wouldn't happen without them reaching out and getting to know each other. She had a feeling it might not be easy for either of them to give up big pieces of themselves too quickly.

She hoped to buy herself time as she thought it through. "What's wrong with getting all mushy?"

Cooper fixed her with a laser stare, the effect of which was offset by the wicked gleam in his eye. "You asked for it."

Firm lips locked with gentle ones, leaving Molly gasping for air. Cooper's hand stilled in her hair and, with a final tug on her locks, joined his other hand on her back. His grip threatened to squeeze her last breath out of her, and Molly reeled in the fierceness of his possession. She surrendered, happily.

As Cooper's mouth left a trail of fire across her lips, her cheek, her ear, the tension Molly had felt all morning at work went in a completely different direction, leaving her on the verge of exploding. He moved on to her neck, exploring at leisure, before stilling and moving back to her lips. When she went on tiptoe to mirror the path he'd taken, starting with his face, he brushed a final kiss across her lips and then took a slight, but noticeable, step backward. Puzzled, Molly stared at him, wondering what she'd done wrong.

Answering her unspoken question, Cooper continued to hold her, but his hands stilled on her back. "You know perfectly well I'd love to do that all day. And all night, although I'd take it indoors and up to your bed, if that's what you want. But you've got a couple of kids who aren't known for their ability to stay in their rooms, and I'm standing outside with you, in front of God and everyone. I'm guessing that's not how you want to make a splash in this neighborhood."

Cheeks flaming, Molly realized what she might've done, given half the chance. Problem was, she never *was* given half the chance, or any other fraction of it.

Recovering, she opted for Plan B. "You said you wanted to talk. About my problems at work, or is something wrong here, too?" The sudden thought of troubles with Alec or Emma, coupled with the strange apathy they'd each shown her today, left her with more worries than she'd brought home.

Tracing his finger down the crease in the middle of her forehead, Cooper gazed at her. "Now, cut it out. Nothing to worry about. I just wanted to talk, starting with what's going on with you and your job, and maybe moving on to other stuff."

Her frown line refused to disappear, but Molly decided a conversation might improve her mood. It couldn't possibly make it worse, right? "I'm game. The thing is, it's still up in the air at work. I didn't mean to shut you out before, but I wanted to get away from it for a few hours. It wasn't about you."

Cooper shrugged. "I shouldn't have gotten upset. I'm the same way sometimes, and I don't know how to back off."

Molly appreciated his candor but was a little unnerved at the idea of receiving more of it. She still preferred to avoid, if she could, an in-depth analysis of her job situation.

"Tell you what. I haven't talked about much *other* than my stupid job in the last few weeks. Why don't you . . . hmmm . . . tell me what you want to be when you grow up?" Waving her index finger at him, she continued on. "And don't give me any garbage about wanting to be a nanny. What would your dream job be?"

She'd thrown him a curveball, if the stunned look on his face was any hint. Cooper didn't speak for a few moments.

"Geez. I don't know. Not that I don't want to spend the rest of my life playing with your kids, but . . ." He grinned for effect, then slowly nodded. "A toy store. Stupid, huh? I've always wanted to have my own business, and hanging out with the little guys crystallized it for me. I can't believe the cool stuff they have nowadays, so it'd be fun, but it would also let me do the ownership thing. I'd love that."

"Really? What —"

Molly's response was interrupted by Cooper's return volley. "Sorry, but no questions. My turn. What's your dream job?"

Even though she'd started it, Molly had no response. Until everything started happening with Jed at work, she'd thought she already had her dream job. Was it time to give up that dream? Shaking her head, she realized she wasn't ready to decide.

"Oh, I —" Hearing the front doorbell, Molly pulled out of Cooper's relaxed hold on her and hurried inside to greet the unexpected caller. Probably someone selling something. Thank God she didn't have to deal with that most days.

Opening the door, Molly plastered a fake smile on her face in case it was a neighbor, not a solicitor. "What can I —"

"Hello, Molly." Casting furtive glances to

each side of him, Jed Parker stood on her
front doorstep, hat in hand. Literally.

CHAPTER TWELVE

"Jed." It amazed Molly that she could form even a single word. Her brain went limp at the sight of her boss. Speech eluded her.

She'd never seen Jed looking like this. He always wore the most dapper, elegant clothes for every occasion — if anything, too much so for Molly's taste, but it wasn't unusual in the retail world. Gold watch, diamond cuff links, too many rings, and other assorted jewelry. Now in his fifties, Jed wore his age well, too, with the graying temples on his otherwise dark brown, ultra-coiffed hair the only obvious sign that time was passing.

Today, he looked like hell. His stained, rumpled slacks looked like he'd gardened in them. Hair askew, eyes glassy, it was no wonder his shirt was wrinkled and only half tucked in. No belt. A dirty Minnesota Twins baseball cap crumpled in one hand. Unbelievable. He was an unqualified, absolute mess. What on earth happened to him?

Cooper came up behind Molly, which she realized only after Jed's gaze appeared to focus on an apparition over her left shoulder. Jed was nervous when she opened the door, but his face went white at the presence of a third person. For a moment, Molly debated whether to take pity on him and ask Cooper to give them space. She'd ordinarily do it without thought, but right now, Molly didn't mind letting Jed stew.

Jed settled the question. "Look, uh, is there anywhere we could talk? Alone?" He croaked out the last word in a fair imitation of a pubescent fourteen-year-old boy, rather than a man with forty more years on his voice.

For once in her life, Molly didn't feel like competing for a hospitality award. "That depends. What do you think we need to discuss?" Glancing over her shoulder, she saw Cooper standing, arms crossed, superbly playing the role of a lawyer. Her lawyer. She owed it to Jed to give him the time alone, and she could handle this on her own, but it felt good having Cooper behind her. Ready to defend.

"Molly. Five minutes. That's all I ask. Can't I get that after all I've done for you?" His eyes beseeched her while darting frequently to Cooper, who moved to her side.

Molly snorted at his desperate play for gratitude. "Jed, I —"

"Hey, who's the guy? What's he doing here?" Jed spoke as if Cooper weren't present, or couldn't hear if he were. At least some things never changed. Jed had always been known for his sales savvy, not his ability to manage people.

Molly involuntarily flushed, thinking back to the recent moments in Cooper's arms. Reminding herself why Jed must be here, she recovered and stood straighter, taller.

"Not that it's any of your business, Jed, but Cooper is my nanny. For my kids." Her unnecessary clarification irritated her. She needed to be sharp, crisp, in control. Not stumble. And, ultimately, win whatever battle Jed was waging against her.

"Really? Well, could you ask him to leave us alone?" Jed's entreaty was as close as he ever got to begging. Molly saw it as a positive development.

"Cooper, could you give us a few minutes? We'll use my office." Molly exchanged a knowing look with Cooper over her choice of turf and assured him with her eyes that she'd manage just fine on her own. She had to.

Cooper silently spun on his heels and

walked into the kitchen, whistling tunelessly as he went. Waving her hand in the direction of her home office, a small paneled room tucked to one side of the living room, Molly moved toward it and ushered Jed in the door. To strike a balance between Jed's request for privacy and her subconscious fear of . . . who knew what, she left the door slightly ajar, but not so much that Jed should notice. No matter what, she couldn't afford to appear weak.

Her office was as good as it got for a meeting like this. She knew Cooper realized it instinctively, perhaps from his years spent maneuvering for every advantage he could over his opponents. A large window took up almost all the space on the outside wall of the small room, and Molly's large, raised leather chair faced that window. The view outside never failed to calm her.

The only other seat in the room was the loveseat, covered in a plum paisley fabric and notable for how low to the floor its occupants had to sit. The kids loved it. Right now, the sight of Jed on it amused her, but she acknowledged it with only a faint flicker of a smile. She couldn't care less if Jed noticed.

She needn't have worried. Slumped down on the loveseat, Jed clasped his hands between his knees and stared at the floor as if the diamond pattern in the blue oriental rug were the most intriguing sight he'd witnessed in years.

Much more of this, and she'd start to pity him. No way. "So? What brings you here in the middle of the afternoon? Or anytime, for that matter?"

"You've heard. You always were a quick one, Molly."

Leaning over her desk, elbows on it and hands cupping her chin, Molly somehow resisted rolling her eyes. "It's a little late for flattery. But just to make sure we have this straight, why don't you tell me what you think I've heard?"

With Greta's latest analysis of the numbers still unclear, at least to Molly, she hoped he couldn't see through her. She needed to get the full story from someone, even if it was the person gunning for her.

Jed's eyes took in the whole room, bouncing from lamp to knickknack to ceiling tile and back again. Everything in the room but Molly, who primly folded her hands on top of the desk. Even after driving all the way here to talk, he wasn't quite ready for this. Fine. She was prepared to wait.

At last, his gaze landed on her, but he still didn't look her straight in the eye. Confession time, she hoped. Clearing his throat a dozen times, Jed's discomfort grew with the passing moments. Molly considered offering him a glass of water, but it was more likely an attack of conscience than anything in his throat. She leveled a cool stare at him, calmly watching as beads of sweat broke out on his forehead before trickling into his eyes. He blinked but did nothing to stop them.

"I'm waiting."

As if snapped out of a trance, Jed shook his head. "Molly. I have no idea how to tell you this. I'll make it up to you, swear to God. Somehow."

So much for a five-minute conversation. At the rate this was going, her kids would eventually join them for a pajama party.

"Why don't you start at the beginning? That usually works."

"Yes. Yes, I'll do that." Jed's eyes dropped from Molly's face, returning to focus again on the floor. Molly made a mental note to vacuum it one of these days.

"God, this is embarrassing. I've been a fool. A stupid, arrogant, gullible fool." Jed's voice again cracked, his anguish provoking Molly's compassion for the man who, according to Greta, was out to destroy her. Steeling her resolve, she didn't let her face reflect her feelings.

"Why? What makes you say that?" Jed's description of himself, with the possible exception of arrogant, wasn't exactly typical. Far from it. Jed was a smart, capable man. Despite his recent oddities, he remained a success by every measure. Even his few detractors within the company — and everyone had some — admitted it.

"What do *you* think of a man who decided he'd earned his right to his first fling, only to have it blow up in his face?"

Molly still shook at the wild tale she'd heard. After relaying it, Jed slunk out of her house, promising to return to the office only to tender his resignation after more than twenty years with Harrowby's.

Cutting through all of Jed's hesitations, stammering, and backtracking, Molly gleaned the bare essentials of what had happened. Someone would have to fill in a few blanks, but for now she was satisfied. And relieved.

Susie Dixon, the young woman she'd noticed but dismissed on her New York trip, had targeted Jed as her prey. At least to hear *Jed* tell it. He'd aim for the best spin he could get, of course, if any good spin were possible, but Susie sounded grisly by anyone's interpretation. In bed, more than a match for Molly's neighbor, Brooke. Out of bed, words failed to capture the greedy, vengeful, vicious young woman.

For whatever reason, soon after landing an entry-level job in the buying group at Harrowby's upon her college graduation in late May, Susie had fixated on two people. Jed, who would get her to the top, and Molly. In some twisted sort of homage to Molly, Susie saw her as both a role model and the woman to beat. Molly hadn't really noticed Susie in the crowd of summer hires or given her the time of day. Maybe that had triggered the painstaking plot. Who knew? The young woman might be crazy. She was certainly criminal.

For the first few weeks of the tryst, Jed's head had been in the clouds, and he hadn't noticed what was happening. Susie's constant questions fed his ego, made him feel as if his job was the most important at Harrowby's. He had no idea she was using the information to set up an elaborate scheme to rob Harrowby's blind and, in the process, take Molly out.

Molly flinched at the detail that went into Susie's twisted agenda. Was that what they taught people in business school these days?

According to Jed, by the time he came to

his senses enough to see the situation for what it was, Susie had him over a barrel. She'd threatened to tell his wife everything, spill the beans at work, take him down with her. He'd been scared out of his mind. Susie knew it and plumbed it to her advantage.

Now Susie was nowhere to be found, and a few hundred thousand dollars in cash and merchandise were gone. Eventually they'd find her and any remaining scraps of her newfound wealth. In the meantime, Jed's life was in shambles, his wife had changed the locks on the house, and today he'd leave in disgrace from the job he'd loved until his "summer romance" stripped it all away.

Where did it leave Molly? Sure, her job was secure. With Jed gone, she might be in line for a promotion or even get offered his job. Her dreaded confrontation with Jed turned out to be anticlimactic. His problem, not hers.

As she tried to make sense of it all, she felt a pair of arms around her shoulders, pinning her close. Cooper. The five minutes with Jed had turned into forty-five. He'd left, but Molly remained transfixed, glued to the chair in her office. No longer aware of anything else going on in the house.

"Molly. Are you okay?" Cooper's deep baritone washed over her, soothing her as dozens of scattered thoughts wrestled for control of her brain.

Spinning around in her chair, she looked up at Cooper, who let go of her and stood, leaning over her, one hand propped on the desk.

"Where are Emma and Alec?" Part of her needed to talk, part sought the comfort and distraction of two adorable little children who wouldn't care if someone bled money from Harrowby's and helped destroy a marriage. Not that she blamed it all on Susie. She felt a little sorry for Jed, but he was the idiot who let this happen.

Cooper propped one hip on the edge of the desk, clasping his hands around his bent knee. "Still down for the count. I heard stirrings a few minutes ago, then nothing. Won't be long before they're up."

"Oh." Molly's brain still functioned on slow speed, if not in reverse.

"What happened? I almost interrupted when it went so long, but I figured you'd shout if you needed me. Are you still employed? Is that why your boss showed up?"

Cooper was definitely headed in the wrong direction on that one. She didn't feel like rehashing it, not yet, but she could ease his immediate concerns. "No, nothing like that. The opposite. Bottom line, Jed had his first and probably last affair. His unlucky choice aimed to rob us blind and, for some reason, take me down with her. I still don't know why. Anyway, Jed's the one who'll be leaving Harrowby's, not me. At least, not yet."

Cooper's eyes narrowed at the quick play-by-play. It obviously wasn't what he expected. He started to speak, then broke off and began again. "Wait. What do you mean, not yet? Why would you leave after all that's happened?"

"No, you're right. I'm still processing it all. I . . ." Trailing off, Molly let her mind drift. For once, she didn't force herself to wrap everything up in a neat and precise package.

Squeals interrupted her train of thought, and two little bodies tumbled into the room. Emma landed on Molly's lap, while Alec tackled Cooper around the waist, sending papers flying off Molly's desk. The nap had greatly improved Alec's disposition, much to Molly's relief. From a foot away, he shouted at her. "Mommy! Do you wanna play? I got something to show you."

Tugging at her hand, Alec pushed Emma out of the way and forced Molly to stand. He then dragged her out of the room. Laughing, she called back to Cooper. "Sorry. Prior engagement. I just hope it's not a dead animal. Or a live one, either."

Cooper, with Emma in his arms, followed close behind. The four proceeded to the tree house, Alec leading the way. Despite her work clothes, she managed to climb up the ladder and was soon holding, gingerly and with a scrunched nose, a beetle the size of a golf ball.

Molly deposited the bug into Cooper's outstretched hand. Wasn't that what she paid him for? She hoped he understood the look they'd exchanged and would somehow manage to remove the bug from her vicinity, with Alec none the wiser. Sometimes, being a mom was absolutely disgusting.

No. With Alec, most of the time.

Still dressed in her work clothes, she didn't know what to do with her hands. Ew. She needed to get inside to change and wash up. Maybe fumigate her hands. "Hey, guys, if we're going to attack any more live creatures, I've got to do something about these clothes. But, first, how about if I take tomorrow off? We could —"

"Yaaay!" Emma and Alec shouted in unison, clapping their chubby little hands.

"Good! I thought we could plan a nice day. Go to the children's museum, then library hour and maybe lunch at the Malt Shop. After your naps, we could drive to

Stillwater and see the boats, maybe shop." At the sight of two small pairs of shoulders drooping as her list continued, she revised it. "Okay, maybe we shop at the *toy* store there. The one you love. Wouldn't that be fun?"

Silence greeted her enthusiastic plan. Dead silence, even from Cooper. Were the children still tired from their naps? They'd been so excited only moments ago.

Emma broke the silence. "Gee, Mommy, could we just stay home?"

Molly looked from one small blond head to the other. The happy grins on Alec's and Emma's faces were long gone. Alec scuffed one toe against the ground.

Cooper provided the color commentary, but Molly wasn't thrilled to hear it. "It's not that they wouldn't enjoy a day like that, Moll. They'd just rather figure it out as the day goes along. Schedules like that were part of what drove me from law. Could we be spontaneous?"

Molly winced at the sight of two small heads nodding in unison at Cooper's words. Why wasn't anyone ever on her side anymore?

Momentarily frustrated, and emotionally overwhelmed at all that had happened today, she snapped. "Fine. We'll do spontaneous. How does eight o'clock tomorrow sound, or would that cut into everyone's sense of spontaneity?"

She whirled and went back to the house. No one had to tell her she was acting childishly. It was her turn.

Twenty-four hours made a big difference. Starting bright and early the next morning, Alec and Emma went on overdrive. With two adults to minister to their every need, they ran Molly and Cooper in circles. They even managed to accomplish half of Molly's original agenda, but spaced in between tree climbing, wading in the creek, and chasing butterflies, the day had an entirely different flavor from what Molly had envisioned.

It was a lot better.

Just after four o'clock, Molly relaxed in the shade of the elm tree in the backyard as Cooper splashed with the twins in the pool. Life felt great. Her entire world had nearly crashed on her yesterday, and today she couldn't be happier. Things weren't what she could call settled with Cooper — far from it — but without the tension at work, maybe she could relax and see where things went with him.

As that thought fluttered through her mind, Cooper glanced over at her from the pool, catching her eye. She smiled. He would never fit her image of a nanny, but maybe that wasn't the biggest deal in the world. Her kids had a blast with him. Soon enough, they'd be in school, contending with schedules and increasingly complex lives.

And then what? Would Cooper fade into history, go back to his firm, move on to someone else? That was what she'd expected all along, wasn't it? With the closeness they'd shared, she liked the thought less than ever.

"Yoohoo! Cooper! Could you come over here for one teensy little moment?" Molly turned her head to see Brooke, in a filmy slip of a bikini, waving her hand as she chirped in her falsetto at Cooper. Just what Molly needed. A reminder of exactly what might take Cooper away from her.

Molly picked up her book and pretended to read, not wanting to interfere in Cooper's choice. Besides, she'd rather find out sooner than later.

"Sorry, Brooke, but I'm busy." Out of the corner of her eye, Molly saw Cooper look from her to Brooke. Probably trying to decide which one he preferred. She burned in mortification, knowing the ultimate decision he'd make.

Brooke waved at Cooper, ever more frantically. Glancing again at Brooke, Molly realized that Brooke must not see her. Even Brooke would tone it down if she knew Molly was there to catch her act. Wouldn't she? Or were she and Cooper already an item?

"Oh, the kids will be fine. I won't keep you long. I just need a little *help* with something. Please, Cooper?" Her high-pitched voice, accompanied by that outrageous swimsuit, was getting to Molly. She may as well lose him now as later. Looking up from her book, she nodded to Cooper but said nothing.

At his quizzical look, she nodded again.

Cooper climbed out of the pool, leaving Emma and Alec splashing happily in the shallow end. Molly could swear she heard a squeal out of Brooke at the sight of her prey. Did grown women really squeal? She didn't want to know.

Molly followed Cooper with her eyes as he trudged through the gate in the fence dividing the two yards. Brooke still didn't notice her. Small wonder. The woman had her sights set on Cooper, and Cooper alone.

Rising, Molly knelt on her lawn chair to get a better view without being too obvious. Not good enough. She wanted to hear this as much as see it. She needed to know now, before she got in deeper. Sliding out of the lawn chair, she bent low and crept to the fence. Keeping her head below the top of it, she glanced behind her to check on the kids, then peeked into Brooke's yard through the slats in the wood.

Just in time to see Brooke fling off her bikini top and throw her arms around Cooper.

Molly staggered backward, knees buckling, as she realized the extent of Cooper's relationship with Brooke. She didn't need to watch. It would only add salt to the wound. She'd —

"Good grief, Brooke. What on earth is the matter with you? Have you lost your mind?" At Cooper's livid shout, Molly turned back to the fence and stole another peek through the slats.

Brooke's arms were no longer around Cooper, who still faced her, but with hands jammed on his hips. She licked her lips and refused to cover herself. "Oh, Cooper, baby, have a little fun. I'm all yours. I *want* you. Every single inch of you, if you know what I mean."

"Spare me. And put some clothes on. Geez." Cooper hadn't taken his hands off his hips. He stood there, still facing Brooke.

Molly chewed her fingernails.

Brooke was undaunted. "I know you must want me. Who else? Poor little Molly, with her precious little children? That would be the day."

"Right. Poor little Molly. As if . . ."

At his words, Molly felt sick. Her stomach roiled and clenched, threatening to send up whatever she'd eaten for lunch. Cooper might not want Brooke, but he didn't want Molly either. Behind her back, he even called her "poor little Molly" just like Brooke did. They probably —

". . . as if anything about her was little. Except maybe her ego, which is on the small side for such a talented woman. You're nothing like Molly, Brooke, but don't take that as a compliment. I don't just want Molly. I'm . . . in love with her, not that it's any of your business. She's the first woman I've *ever* loved."

"We —"

With a slash of his hand, Cooper cut off Brooke's response. "There is no 'we.' Get over it. Save your charms for someone who can stomach them."

Turning his head back to Molly's yard, he stormed across the lawn, then slammed the gate behind him. Only to see Molly, crouched down beside the fence, a mere five feet away.

"Molly, I —"

"No, Cooper. I believe it's 'we.' "

Pulling her to her full height and grabbing her around the waist, he lifted her up in the air, twirling in a circle. "Sorry, but for once in your life, you're wrong. There *is* an 'I.' It's I who loves you." Setting her back down, he captured her lips with a kiss that promised her forever.

EPILOGUE

"Mommy! Coop! It's three o'clock! Time to go!" The very grown-up Emma, now in kindergarten, looked at her new Mickey Mouse watch for the tenth time in the same number of minutes.

Tossing her in the air a few times before finally setting her down, Cooper laughed at her shrieks. Dressed in satin and bows for the christening, she tried without success to maintain a solemn look as she wagged her finger at Cooper. She couldn't hide her delight. As the official big sister on this glorious day, she was enjoying almost more attention than the twins.

The twins. Fate had struck Molly again, Cooper thought, not for the first time. Picking up his baby son, he nuzzled his nose in tiny Josh's face and stole a peek over Molly's shoulder at Grace.

On the other hand, knowing Molly, she was just being her usual efficient self. Leave it to Molly to produce in two tries what it took other women four. Some things never changed. Smiling at the woman he loved more every day, Cooper imitated Josh's coos and gurgles and pretended to wince as Josh grabbed his finger.

"If you think *that* kid is tough, don't forget his sister. Grace is going to win the Golden Glove, if that pummeling I took means anything." Clapping Cooper on the back, Molly's brother, Steve, relieved him of his small bundle. Stopping short of tossing Josh in the air, Steve laughed at Cooper's horrified expression. "Oh, calm down. Just giving you a hard time. Aren't you the same guy who used to hang Emma upside down from the tree house? Weren't you that wild nanny, or am I thinking of another one?"

Playing musical babies, Cooper retrieved Grace from Molly, leaving her to seek out a five-year-old twin if she wanted a cuddle. "Yeah, that was me, all right. I guess times have changed." Throwing his head back, he laughed. "Well, at least for now. I'm just letting these two get a few more months on them before they start swinging from trees. Can't you give me that?"

Letting Josh suck on his finger, Steve nodded. "Sounds fair. After all, I'm supposed to take good care of my godchild, aren't I?"

"That you are." Leaving Steve as he made faces and spoke gibberish at Josh, Cooper turned to Molly, now being fiercely hugged and kissed by Alec.

"Have I told you lately how much I love you?" Leaning over, he cradled Grace in one arm as he put his other arm around his wife.

"Not enough." The sizzling look she gave him belied her words. Having recently returned to work as head of retail operations at Harrowby's — Jed's old job — Molly was already complaining about feeling frazzled. But she loved it, and the glow on her face said it all. Juggling four kids, an exciting but demanding job, and a husband had to be tough. Cooper didn't know a lot of women — or men — who could pull it off. The woman of his dreams somehow did. Day after day.

And, more important, she'd given him the time and space to figure out what he wanted to be when he grew up. For that, his love for her threatened to overwhelm him. The grand opening of his new toy store was next Tuesday. A dream come true. Another great folly in a life now full of folly. In a good way.

The only negative? He'd had to give up that cushy job he'd snagged two summers ago. As it turned out, Molly wanted a decent nanny for a change.

Go figure.

ACKNOWLEDGMENTS

My huge thanks to:

Jenny Crusie, who taught the very first writing workshop I ever attended and made light bulbs go off and my head spin, all in a good way.

Chris Lashinski and Vicki Jadwinski, who long ago critiqued my first draft for the Golden Heart contest and didn't tell me (at the time) how many hilarious mistakes I made.

Melissa McClone, who kicked my butt (lovingly) until I sold this book.

Barbara Samuel, who teaches a fabulous writers' voice class and hasn't yet resigned as my mentor, which either qualifies her for a courage award or makes her judgment somewhat suspect.

261

All the fabulous peeps at Bell Bridge Books, especially Deb Dixon, who said "send it," Deb Smith, who said "we'll buy it," and Danielle Childers, who introduced me to white-chocolate pickles.

Ann Burns, my first reader on all my books, who always tells me she loves them no matter what she may privately think.

Michael Bodine, who helped me hang in there until this happened and never made fun of my impatience . . . except on days ending in "y."

Morganna Starrett, who helps my computer hang in there no matter what I do to it, and Liz Selvig, who worked miracles teaching me (as best she could, considering her student) how to do a website.

The Goalies (Lynn Coddington, Katy Cooper, Deb Dixon, Julie Hurwitz, Jill Limber, Beth Pattillo, and Carol Prescott), who always have my back.

All of my other oodles and oodles of adorable writing friends, including my friends in Romex, especially the Pursuit gang; Midwest Fiction Writers, especially the Club

100 gang; Washington Romance Writers; Just Cherry Writers; and the Princesses (Monica Pradhan Caltabiano, Rosemary Heim, Becky Klang, Chris Lashinski, Tina Plant, Katie Quay, Roxanne Richardson, and Helen Twomey).

ABOUT THE AUTHOR

Mary Strand practiced corporate law in a large Minneapolis law firm for sixteen years until the day she set aside her pointy-toed shoes (or most of them) and escaped the land of mergers and acquisitions to write novels. The first novel she wrote, *Cooper's Folly,* won Romance Writers of America's Golden Heart award. *Cooper's Folly* is her debut novel.

Mary lives on a lake in Minneapolis with her husband, two cute kidlets, and a stuffed monkey named Philip. When not writing, she loves traveling, dancing badly to live music, playing guitar (also badly), and playing sports with reckless abandon and a high probability of injuring herself.

If she has any vices — and she totally denies it — they might include rock bands, triple-berry scones, Five Guys burgers, Cosmopolitans, her adorable little convertible, and Hugh Jackman. She'd rather not say how many chocolate-banana crêpes she eats every time she finagles another trip to Paris. Oh, and she wants to be a rock star when she grows up. If she ever does.

Mary writes romantic comedy, YA, and women's fiction novels. You can find her at www.marystrand.com, follow her on Twitter (@Mary_Strand), or "like" her on Facebook:
(www.facebook.com/marystrandauthor)